Aron's Element

Aron's Element

Lynn Howard
@2020
Published by Twisted Heart Press, LLC

Chapter One

Tires crunched on gravel, and Charlie's anxiety kicked up a few notches. She knew who it was. Or at least she knew it would be a member of the Ravenwood Pride coming to check on her as they'd done the last six weeks since she'd been almost taken by rogue Shifters.

Six weeks. It had been six weeks since the last time she'd left her house. Six weeks since the nightmares had started. Six weeks that she'd struggled to get back to who she was.

As much as she hated depending on the panthers, she still couldn't bring herself to go into public. While the panthers were Shifters, just like the ones who'd taken her, they had proven to her, both that night and since, they were the good guys. They acted like they truly cared about Charlie and her welfare.

Maybe they did.

The first few times they'd pulled up her long driveway and parked in front of her small ranch home she'd feared them, feared their intentions. But little by little, they'd burrowed themselves into her heart.

Especially Aron.

Aron was the Alpha of the Ravenwood Pride and seemed to be the one who showed up the most. Charlie tried to convince herself it was because he was the head of the Pride, that he'd made it his own personal mission to ensure Charlie didn't tell anyone what had happened that night to protect the secret of the existence.

But she knew that wasn't true.

Charlie was an Elemental Fairy. The panthers knew she had no desire to let anyone know about their existence any more than she wanted humans to know about her own. Humans tended to fear the unknown. They wouldn't welcome all the non-humans of the world with open arms. They'd try to capture them and experiment on them. They would try to eliminate them for fear of being taken over.

The vehicle stopped next to her little Audi, she assumed, the engine idling for a few minutes. Finally, the driver turned off his truck, opened the door, and made his way to Charlie's front porch.

She knew by the sound of the vehicle, as well as the cadence of his steps, it was Aron out there.

She also knew he wouldn't come to the front door. He wouldn't even step onto the first step of her porch. He always waited at the bottom for her to come out, always waited for her to decide whether she wanted to talk to him.

Pulling a blanket around her shoulders, she padded barefoot to the front of her house and opened the door.

"Hey," he said, his eyes dropping immediately.

When Aron had first started coming around, she wondered if he didn't like her. He refused to come onto the porch, refused to come into her house, and barely looked her in the eye.

But then she'd noticed it was the same with all the panthers. The only time any of them had touched her was when she was first brought home. As she had climbed from the back cab of Braxton's truck, she'd stumbled and almost fell. He had reached out, grabbed her arm to steady her, then immediately stepped back.

That was it. Other than Campbell's periodic hugs, there had been no physical interaction between herself and the panthers.

"Hey," she said back when she realized how long she'd stood there staring at him as he stared at his boots.

His eyes raised to her face, dropped, then did a double take. They narrowed on her face and she felt like he was seeing straight to her soul for a second.

"Still not sleeping well?" he asked.

She had lied every single time anyone had asked her that question. They all asked the same questions: *How are you sleeping? Are you eating okay?*

And she always said she was fine.

But as Aron watched her expectantly, she didn't have the energy to lie. Not anymore. Not to him.

"No," she said, then sighed. It was like she had released some weird control the nightmares had over her by admitting that out loud.

He nodded. "Is your appetite back?"

If she hadn't had the blanket wrapped around her like a shield, he would've been able to see how much weight she'd lost over the past month and a half.

"Not really."

"When was the last time you got out? When was the last time you got a real meal in your system?"

Charlie's brows hit her hairline. He knew the answer to the first question – the panthers had been bringing her groceries and other supplies the whole time. And she'd already admitted she didn't have much of an appetite.

"I haven't gone anywhere since that night."

It was irrational, this fear of leaving her home. The Rogues had found her on her own property. She'd been wandering the woods behind her house in what she liked to call her meditation time. Not that she really knew how to meditate, but it was how she relaxed, by reconnecting with nature.

Charlie had had only a split second to react before arms clamped down around her and she was hit in the head. It had knocked her senseless enough she wasn't able to use her wind magic to protect herself.

At the time, it had felt like they'd dragged her for hours through the woods. But when the panthers had shown up and taken her home, she'd been surprised to find they were only about a mile or two from where she'd been taken.

Even though she'd been taken from her own backyard, she found it hard to step foot outside without one of the panthers there. She no longer went for her meditation walks. She didn't even drink her coffee on the front porch anymore.

"Are you hungry now?" Aron asked.

Was she hungry? She had hunger pangs here and there, but the thought of food made her stomach turn.

"I won't let anyone hurt you. I promise. I swear on my own life."

That small statement held so much that Charlie's heart kicked up a notch.

She had zero doubt the panthers would protect her. She had zero doubt Aron could keep her safe. But the way Aron said it sounded like he'd lay down his life for her. And that was something she could never ask from anyone.

Wait. Was he promising to protect her because he expected her to leave?

"Where do you want to go?"

She could probably handle hanging out with the panthers at one of their houses. She'd never been super comfortable around Shifters, but this group was different. They'd endured injuries to protect her. They'd made sure she was getting through the trauma of almost being sold off as a breeder to some sick, twisted Rogue.

"A friend of ours owns a place. It's a..." He swallowed. "It's a Shifter bar. But it's safe. I swear I'll keep you safe."

A Shifter bar. A bar full of Shifters. The Pride was one thing, but a whole other group of people like the ones who'd taken her?

And then Charlie realized since the first word she'd spoken to Aron today, he hadn't dropped his eyes to the ground once. He was watching her. Studying her. Pleading with his eyes for her to trust him.

And she wanted to. Oh, how she wanted to. She wanted to get back to living life. She wanted to get back among the living. She'd moved to this town, to this house in hopes of meeting someone, falling madly in love, and filling the house with kids.

No way in hell was she going to let a group of assholes ruin her life, her plans, and her future.

"Okay," she said.

Aron blinked and his head jerked back the slightest bit as if her answer had surprised him.

"Give me a second."

A ghost of a smile tilted the corners of Aron's lips up and Charlie realized that was the closest to a smile she'd seen on him since she'd met him. The other guys in his Pride were rougher looking with long or shaggy hair, tattoos, and piercings.

Aron had short, dark blonde hair and not a tattoo or piercing she could see.

And she suddenly found herself wanting to know if there were any hidden beneath his clothes.

Shaking her head to get the thought out – she had no right fantasizing about Aron – she turned and jogged into the house. As much as she'd love to leave the house wearing the comfy sweats, threadbare t-shirt, and blanket shawl, she needed to at least look as if she were trying.

Charlie tossed her dirty clothes in the hamper and hastily pulled on a pair of jeans and a clean t-shirt and grabbed a sweater for when the temperature dropped later. Shoving her feet into a pair of sandals, she checked her reflection in the mirror hanging above her dresser.

She was a mess. Dark lavender crescents underlined her eyes; her skin looked pallid and dull. And she definitely needed to drag a brush through her hair before going anywhere.

As Charlie brushed out the knots in her hair, a small wave of embarrassment hit her. She'd stood on the porch looking like a bum while Aron was perfect as usual. His hair was always perfectly combed, his clothes fit him as if they'd been made for him. Even his shoes were free of dirt or scuffs.

With a sigh, Charlie set her brush on her dresser and frowned at herself. It didn't matter how he looked or how *she* looked. Eventually, the Pride would go back to their normal lives and forget she existed. And she would get back to her normal life. It wouldn't help her to develop a crush on Aron.

With one more frustrated sigh, she twisted her hair out of her face with a ponytail holder and headed outside.

One of the panthers, Daxon, had installed new locks on both front and back doors as well as ensuring her window locks were secure. While they all knew doors and windows couldn't keep a Shifter out if they really wanted in, it would give her time to call for help if someone showed up to finish the job the Rogues failed.

Turning all three deadbolts in place with a key, she turned to find Aron standing in the same place as she'd left him. His arms were crossed over his chest and he seemed to be watching her property, watching over her while she was inside.

His eyes jerked to her face when she stepped through the screen door then did a slow perusal of her body from head to toe.

The faintest glow entered his irises as they raised back up to her face. His mouth opened, then closed without a word being uttered.

Charlie looked down at herself. Maybe she should change. But he was wearing jeans and t-shirt, too. Why should she dress up when she was already nervous as can be about reentering society?

The glow in Aron's eyes flashed brighter then faded as he took a deep breath in through his nose and blew it out through his mouth in a rush. "You ready?" he asked.

Was his voice deeper than normal? It sure sounded that way to Charlie. But she had no idea what the combination of the glow in his eyes and the soft growl in his words meant.

But she wasn't scared. Not of Aron. Never of Aron.

He walked ahead of her, pulling the passenger door open and stepping out of the way. Even as Charlie struggled to climb into his humongous truck, he never offered his hand, never moved forward to give her a push inside.

Why did he refuse to touch her? Did he realize she was attracted to him and was trying to avoid hurting her feelings when he had to refuse her advances? It wasn't like she planned to act on her crush.

Once Charlie was in her seat and buckled in, Aron pushed the door closed and rounded the hood, glancing up at her once as he passed.

"How far is the bar?" Charlie asked when Aron was in his seat and the truck was pulling down her driveway.

"Not far. About fifteen minutes," he said.

And then the cab went quiet except the soft music playing in the background.

She wanted Aron to talk. She wanted something to focus on other than the growing anxiety as they moved further and further from her safe little bubble. But she had no idea what to say to start the conversation.

The fifteen minutes it took to get to a one-story, unassuming white building with several trucks and cars parked in the gravel lot gave her mind plenty of time to work up every worst case scenario possible. Sweat rolled down her back and her heart raced in her chest to the point she knew Aron had to be able to hear it.

"You'll be safe. I texted the rest of the Pride while you were getting ready. They're in there waiting for us," he said, nodding his head toward the front door where Campbell stood, a smile on her face as she lifted one hand in greeting.

"I'll be safe," she repeated, staring into Aron's pale green eyes.

"You'll be safe."

His hand raised and moved toward her, but he jerked it back and frowned down at it as if he'd had no control over the movement.

Pushing from his door, he slammed it closed before rounding the hood and opening hers. He stood beside the door, his eyes once again dropping to the ground a second after making contact with hers.

And they were back to that.

For some reason, she had thought they'd had some weird friendship breakthrough back at her house. But he simply felt responsible for her since he had helped her with the Rogues.

8

Charlie climbed from her seat and stood beside the door as he closed and locked it. But she couldn't make her feet move forward, even when he started walking away.

Aron glanced back, forward, then back at her when he realized she wasn't walking with him.

Campbell still waited by the front door, and he'd said the panthers were inside. But the fear and anxiety were freezing her feet right there in the gravel.

"I don't think I can do this," she whispered when he neared her.

Aron bent his knees a little so they were almost eye to eye. "Trust me," he said, lowering his chin a bit. "You know none of us would let anything happen to you. Trust me," he said again.

His hand reached forward and Charlie felt her eyes widen. He was going to touch her? He was offering his hand to her, offering her his strength.

Without another thought, she slipped her hand into his and let him guide her toward the building. His hand was warm, gentle, yet calloused. And so strong. His grip was soft enough to not hurt her but firm enough she felt safe and secure.

Why was he touching her now? This was literally the first time he'd touched her, the first time he'd even come close enough to touch her.

Didn't matter. The reasons didn't matter. What mattered was she swore she could feel her magic reaching for him. It felt as if her magic was trying to wrap itself around him, trying to claim him.

And that wasn't something she could allow. She refused to be some character in one of those unrequited love stories.

"Hey," Campbell said, wrapping an arm around Charlie's free shoulder, but not before shooting Charlie's and Aron's clasped hands a confused frown. It was there and gone so fast Charlie wondered if she'd imagined it. "Everyone's waiting inside."

"Everyone?" Aron said.

Why did he sound worried? He'd already told her he had texted all the panthers and invited them out for dinner.

When Campbell pulled the door open, the scent of stale beer and old cigarette smoke assailed her nose. The low thrum of conversation was barely louder than the country music playing from speakers somewhere in the ceiling.

The conversation all but ceased when Charlie, Aron, and Campbell walked through the door.

"Son of a bitch," Aron muttered under his breath.

The room was packed. And almost everyone was looking at her.

Glancing over her shoulder, she looked for Aron. He was barely a foot behind her, guarding her, shielding her, his hand still clasping hers. When he nodded and actually gave her a small smile of support, Charlie pushed back her shoulders and called forth the strength she'd had her whole life before that night.

She could do this. She was an Elemental Fae. She might not have teeth and claws, but she could fling someone across the room if need be. And she had Aron behind her. She believed him when he said he'd keep her safe.

She trusted him.

****

Aron pulled his eyes from Charlie's ass a half second before she turned to look at him. He felt like a dick. He shouldn't be ogling her, not when she was fighting tooth and nail to get back to normal.

In all honesty, he hadn't been able to get her out of his head since the night his Pride had found her fighting off six male Shifters.

She was striking. And beautiful. And obviously strong, even if she didn't feel it at the moment. Her pale blonde, almost white hair made her light blue eyes haunting. Her eyes tilted down slightly, and her lips were pouty. Even with her lighter features, everything combined gave her a sultry appeal.

And Aron wanted her more than he'd ever wanted another female in his whole damn life.

But she was off limits. She was a victim they were charged to keep safe and help get back to her life. Just like they did with every other female they saved. All he was supposed to do was check on her, make sure she hadn't spoken of the Shifters to anyone else, and make sure she was healing from her ordeal.

That was it.

Instead, he had obsessed over her day and night. Even patrolled her property at night to make sure no one had snuck back to try to grab her again.

He was convinced the jackasses who'd taken her had had no idea she was anything other than human. They'd believed they had wandered upon a helpless human woman. He would've loved to see the looks on their faces when she started using her gift and slinging them all over the woods.

Those aforementioned assholes were dead, rotting in the woods. Unless their buddies had found them. Even that didn't keep Aron from constantly making sure no one else wandered onto her property.

Did the rest of the Pride know how much he snuck off at night?

If they did, no one had said shit to him about it. But he had noticed no one was touching her or making prolonged eye contact other than Campbell. And she wasn't a panther. She didn't follow the same rules his kind or his Pride followed.

As Aron followed Charlie and Campbell into Moe's, her small hand cradled in his, he wondered if she had noticed the lack of affection, hugging, or any form of physical contact.

And even more importantly, did the lack of contact from his Pride brothers mean they'd noticed his feelings toward her? He'd never vocalized them, but that didn't mean a whole lot.

The sounds and smells of the bar filled his senses as Campbell pulled the door open and stepped in ahead of Charlie. Aron released her hand to make room for everyone to enter. Campbell immediately threw her arm around Charlie's shoulders the second they were inside and guided her toward the table where the rest of the panthers and a few other friends sat.

When he'd sent out the text, he'd only meant for his own Pride to show up and give Charlie a sense of security with people she hopefully trusted.

Instead, almost every single wolf from the Big River Pack and the bears from the Blackwater Clan were there, as well as all their mates.

But at least there were a lot of females present. Hopefully, that would put Charlie more at ease when she was surrounded by so many large, dominant Shifters.

"Hi! I'm Nova," the mate to the Alpha of Big River said, standing and reaching for Charlie.

Charlie instantly tensed. Even when Nova wrapped her arms around Charlie's thin body, she never truly relaxed into the hug.

Aron wanted to pull Nova away, to scold her, to ask the rest of his friends to give Charlie space. But that wouldn't help her heal. She needed interaction. She needed to see that Shifters weren't bad people. She needed to feel loved and protected.

"Charlemaine?" a voice called across the bar.

Aron looked up at the bartender, Hollyn, whose eyes were wide as her bottom lip quivered.

Slowly, Hollyn made her way around the bar, shaking her head when her mate and owner of the bar, Noah, asked her what was wrong.

The dark-haired woman took shaky steps toward Charlie, her eyes still wide, her lips moving as if she were trying to say something but nothing would come out.

"Hollynessa?" Charlie asked, the shock evident in her whispered voice.

"How...when...Oh my god!" Hollyn cried out and threw her arms around Charlie.

Charlie instantly hugged her back. The sob that worked up her chest and escaped from

her mouth cut Aron to the core. He assumed those were happy tears streaking down her face, but his panther wanted to burst through and kill whoever had made her cry.

That thought made Aron take a step back. He was supposed to protect her, help her heal. Instead, his animal was already trying to take steps to claim her as his mate.

Nope. He would never do that to a woman who'd gone through the horror she had. He'd never push his feelings on a woman. Would never claim a woman against her will.

He'd rather cut out his own fucking heart.

Moving to stand near his own Pride, Aron watched the women embrace and wondered what the hell was going on. By the looks on everyone else's faces, they were as confused as he was.

"How are you even here?" Hollyn asked, finally pulling back to look into Charlie's face. Neither woman released their grip on each other, like they were scared the other would disappear.

"How are *you* here?" Charlie asked, lifting one hand to wipe the tears from her cheeks.

"I thought you were dead," Hollyn said.

Charlie huffed out a surprised laugh. "Yeah. Same."

They went back to hugging, and Aron shrugged at the raised eyebrows from Campbell and the rest of the panthers.

"Why did they think they were dead?" Reed, a wolf from Big River, said from somewhere behind Aron.

No one spoke. Aron was worried he'd have to beat someone's ass for mentioning the fact both women were Fae in a bar full of people. It was their secret to keep. And the fact both women believed the other dead showed how dangerous their mere existence was for their kind.

"They know each other?" Brax asked from Aron's left.

The women pulled apart and looked toward where everyone sat.

"Charlemaine is my cousin," Hollyn said, her voice thick with emotion. "I haven't seen her in over ten years."

"Charlemaine?" Brax repeated.

"Hollynessa?" Nova said from the table full of wolves and bears and various other Shifters.

"You're totally trying to think of nicknames right now, aren't you?" Reed teased.

But Aron's attention was on the woman who was the physical opposite of her cousin. Where Hollyn's hair was coal black and her eyes were close to the color of sapphire, Charlie's hair was so blonde it looked white. Her skin was pale as were her gray-blue eyes.

But her eyes weren't gray-blue when she turned them to Aron. They were a bright blue, like the color of the sky in Spring. And they were red-rimmed and watery.

The urge to cross the room and pull her into his arms was so strong it about took his damn breath.

What was it about Charlie? He'd helped so many women through the years. He'd checked on dozens on a regular basis for the last five years. Yet this woman was successfully burrowing so deep under his skin he wasn't sure he could ignore his feelings.

It was more than a simple crush, though. He knew without a doubt his panther wanted Charlie as their mate. And as hard as he fucking tried, he couldn't force himself to ignore that declaration.

His panther wasn't the only one who wanted her. Aron wanted her so fucking bad he felt guilty. A relationship was the last thing she needed right now. Especially a relationship with a Shifter.

Why was he even thinking about any of this? She needed his help, not his advances. And he was pretty sure Fairies didn't mate like Shifters did. They fell in love.

Then again…

Noah was a bear Shifter and his mate – who happened to be Charlie's cousin – was an Elemental Fairy. Just like Charlie.

A hand landed on Aron's shoulder and jerked him out of his mental bull shit.

"Did you know they were cousins?" Mason asked.

Aron frowned at him. "How the hell would I know that?"

The Ravenwood Pride panthers had found Hollyn when she'd been taken by rogues. She'd managed to climb out of a window and was running for her life when they'd found her. Mason had kept her safe at the SUV while the rest of them headed back to take out the rogues.

As much as he hated all the killing they'd done over the last five years, he was able to rationalize it. If the assholes were dead, they couldn't steal any more women. They couldn't force animals in them, which could, and often did, end in their deaths.

But even all that rationalizing didn't stop the nightmares most nights.

Hollyn had never mentioned anything about her family when they'd rescued her. They'd watched over her for a couple of weeks before finally depositing her on Noah's front porch. At the time, there were groups aggressively hunting Fairies. The panthers had feared the leader would continue to hunt for Hollyn and figured the safest place for her would be not only in another state, but with the massive bears.

Even if she had mentioned anything about her family, not only did Hollyn believe Charlie dead, they would've had no idea who she was.

Memories of Hollyn's rescue made him wonder. Could the assholes who had taken Charlie have known she wasn't human? Were the rogues back to trying to capture Fae? And if so, they had to know a Fairy couldn't be turned. Forcing an animal into them would kill them instantly. Even a bite from a Shifter would cause their death.

Which meant Aron could never mark Charlie as his own.

Fuck. No matter how hard he tried to push those thoughts away, they constantly came rushing straight to his brain.

Hollyn and Charlie made their way to the table full of friends and sat in two empty spots. And Aron stood behind and over Charlie like a sentry.

There was no reason to be protective of her here. Even though there were males he didn't know, the place was mainly filled with people he'd trust with his own life. They were the people he'd fought beside to get the laws changed regarding female Shifters. They were who he had trusted to keep Hollyn safe when they'd rescued her.

Yet he couldn't make himself leave her side. He stood with his arms crossed over his chest, his eyes raking across the crowd to make sure no one was paying attention to either Charlie or Hollyn.

"What are you doing?" Campbell asked, bumping him with her shoulder as she passed and took a seat between her mate, Brax, and another female from the Blackwater Clan, June.

Campbell knew damn well the panthers wouldn't touch or interact too much with a mated female. It was their way. To them, too much touch or even too much eye contact was disrespectful to the mating bond. But she had done everything she could over the past few months to break that tradition.

Shaking his head, he looked around and realized there were quite a few sets of eyes on him and everyone looked confused. Even leery. He didn't want anyone leery of Charlie. Or Hollyn.

Deciding standing over Charlie like a guard was both ridiculous and drawing unnecessary attention, Aron took the seat beside Brax, positioning him kitty-corner to where Charlie and Hollyn were catching up.

The women constantly hugged each other, always touching one another in what looked to Aron like disbelief. He couldn't imagine the pain of thinking every single member of his family was dead. And that was what both women had gone through for what – years?

Did they have anyone else? Other than Noah and the Clan, did Hollyn have any other surviving family members? What about Charlie? Did she have anyone?

As he watched tears well in her eyes once more, Aron decided this woman needed more than a good meal and a few peaceful nights of sleep. She needed a family.

And he wanted to be that for her more than he wanted his next breath.

Chapter Two

How was this possible? Her cousin was still alive? Charlie had assumed every single member of her family had been slain that night. Yet, Hollynessa sat beside Charlie, her hands wrapped around Charlie's as if they were holding onto a lifeline.

Maybe they were. Charlie almost felt like Hollynessa would disappear the second she released her iron grip.

"I go by Hollyn now," she said, releasing one hand to wipe the tears from her cheek.

"Charlie," she said with a shrug. "Got tired of correcting people when they butchered my name."

Hollyn chuckled and leaned in for yet another hug. "I feel like I'm dreaming."

"I know. Me too," Charlie said, returning the hug.

The whole time Charlie talked to her cousin she was hyper aware of Aron's presence. He'd hovered behind Charlie, an anchor in the sea of chaos she'd just encountered. But then he'd moved to sit in a chair.

Yet he was still within touching distance. Maybe he didn't realize she noticed, but she'd caught him watching her several times.

He was protecting her. That was all. He had promised to keep her safe before they'd left her house. He was making sure she was comfortable in public.

Huh. She hadn't even thought about the fact she was among so many people after hearing Hollynessa – or Hollyn, as she went by now – call her name when she stepped inside this bar. The second she'd seen Hollyn's face, the moment she'd pulled her into a hug, all of Charlie's fears took a backseat.

Maybe not completely. Her fears were still there, but having Hollyn back in her life, knowing she wasn't completely alone, made her feel like maybe she could do this. Maybe she could go back to her life. Maybe she could be the person she was before those assholes wandered onto her property.

But *was* she alone before? Before she'd discovered she still had family on this planet?

As nervous as she was around other people, she'd grown to look forward to the panthers' visits. She'd begun to look forward to Aron's visit most. He was calming. And sweet. Even if he barely looked her in the eye and never came into her home.

She'd invited them all inside at one point or another. Only Campbell accepted.

"What are you doing here?" Hollyn asked, pulling Charlie's thoughts back to the here and now.

Charlie looked over at Aron and wasn't sure how much to tell. They had asked her to keep the abduction to herself, asked her not to report it to the police or let any friends or family know. They had no idea she'd had no family for over a decade. And since she wasn't human, either, she'd had no intention of going to the police. Wasn't like there was much they could do, anyway.

"Same thing as you," Aron answered, glancing at Hollyn as he spoke then looking back to Charlie.

Hollyn turned wide eyes on Charlie. "The rogues? They took you?"

"Almost," Charlie said with a shrug, anticipating the wave of anxiety and terror that came any time she thought about that night.

But it didn't come. As she sat surrounded by her new Shifter friends and her one remaining family member, she remembered her strength.

"She kicked their asses," Campbell said.

Charlie glanced up at Campbell and caught Aron's look of…what? Was that pride in his eyes? The small smile and nod of his head was a definite show of respect. He didn't immediately turn his eyes from hers when she smiled at him.

"You were able to use your…skills?"

All eyes were now on Charlie. The entire table had stopped to listen to her story. And that fear she'd anticipated earlier came rushing through her system, increasing her heart rate and causing sweat to dampen her palms.

While Charlie trusted the panthers, and the Pride obviously trusted the Shifters at the table, there were quite a few other people in the room she didn't know. She had no desire to let every single person in there know she lived with a permanent bull's eye on her back.

Not only would that risk her own life, but Hollyn's, as well.

Looking around the table, she swore she could feel her heart trying to jump out of her chest. For a split second, she was right back in the woods that night. Her fight or flight kicked in and it took every ounce of control to keep from jumping from her chair and running the whole way home.

"She found a big stick and was whooping their asses when we found her. Had them flying all over the place," Aron said, saving Charlie from either giving all her secrets away or making herself look uber suspicious with her silence.

Smiling at Aron, she thanked him with her eyes. He dipped his chin in another short nod. And once again, he didn't turn his eyes away.

When no one started another conversation, Charlie looked around to find everyone looking back and forth between her and Aron.

Heat rushed her cheeks, and she dropped her gaze to the hand still clutching Hollyn's.

"So, how have you been? What have you been doing?" she asked Hollyn.

What she really wanted to ask her cousin was if she knew whether any other family members were still alive. But she didn't want to kill the joyful reunion.

Hollyn told Charlie all about how she'd met her mate and the other bears. She told her about how she'd come to work for Noah even before they'd become so close. She told Charlie all about her new family, her new friends, and how there was a waitress on leave who was carrying what they believed to be a set of twins.

"What about you?" Hollyn asked.

Charlie shrugged. Other than her almost abduction, nothing exciting had happened to her in years. She told Hollyn about how she'd moved from state to state, always careful to avoid large populations of Shifters. She'd had no idea how many lived so closely in this small area.

"You pretty much moved to Shifter Central," Hollyn teased with a jerk of her head toward the packed bar.

Charlie leaned forward and lowered her voice, even though she was sure every single person in there could hear her. Yet, they all averted their eyes and continued on with their conversations, giving the cousins at least a modicum of privacy.

"How have you stayed alive with so many of them around?"

A twinge of guilt hit her heart when she saw the small shake of Aron's head from her periphery. She'd hurt him with her question.

She trusted Aron. She trusted the rest of the panthers and Campbell. But they were a tiny fraction of the population of Shifters in these parts.

"Because every single person at this table and a few who aren't here would rip the throat out of anyone who tried to hurt me," Hollyn whispered back.

Nods around the table. They were all pretending not to listen, but they'd made sure Charlie knew Hollyn was speaking the truth.

Eventually, Charlie began to relax. She couldn't stop touching Hollyn, couldn't stop hugging her and holding her hand. Hollyn's boss also happened to be her mate and never said a word about Hollyn taking the rest of the night off.

In fact, not a single Shifter complained about getting their drinks late with Noah being the only bartender behind the bar.

"He was by himself before Shawnee and I came along. They're used to waiting," Hollyn explained.

Shawnee was the waitress Hollyn had mentioned before. She was mated to a bear and was pregnant with their first baby. Or bab*ies*, according to the rest of the group.

"You'll meet them both eventually. Colton doesn't like to leave her side any more than he has to," Nova, one of the wolves from Big River Pack, explained.

The more she interacted with the large group around the table, the harder it was for her to fear a single one of them. They were all so warm and inviting. Well. One of the guys was intense and tended to stare at her a lot with his bright blue eyes. But Nova explained Micah was the Second in the Big River Pack and tended to be wary of newcomers and overly protective of not only his mate, but the rest of the Pack, as well.

What would Micah think if he found out Charlie was a Fairy? Did he know about Hollyn? Would he fear her? Fear that her presence would bring danger to his family? What about the others?

Being as the entire bar would hear her if she whispered, Charlie decided to wait until they were alone to ask Hollyn if the Shifters knew about her lineage.

As the night wore on, exhaustion began to settle in. It had been weeks since she'd slept more than a few minutes at a time, always waking from nightmares or at the slightest noise. She wanted to get back to who she was before those jerks had come crashing into her life, but she couldn't seem to find her way.

But with Hollyn here, with the new friends she'd found in the panthers, she began to realize she didn't have to do this alone.

Today was the first time she had admitted she was struggling. And Aron hadn't hesitated to get her out of her house and out into the world. He'd called on his friends to help ease her into reality again.

And he'd given her back a part of her family. He might not have done it on purpose, but had he not brought her to Moe's, she would've never known Hollyn was not only alive, but less than twenty minutes from her.

Charlie's jaw cracked as she opened her mouth wide and yawned. Slapping her hand over her mouth, she felt her cheeks go hot as everyone turned to look at her.

"Tired?" Nova teased.

"I should get you home," Aron said from across the table.

She hadn't missed the fact he had stared at her the entire evening, barely interacting with his friends. None of them seemed irritated by his lack of conversation.

Why was he staring at her? Was he nervous for her? Worried someone would hurt her? Everyone else at the table was relaxed. They laughed and joked and teased each other. They included Charlie in on their conversations and made her feel as if she were part of their group.

But Aron just stared.

"Promise you'll come back," Hollyn said, pulling Charlie to her feet and wrapping her arms around her shoulders in a tight embrace.

"I promise," Charlie said against Hollyn's shoulder. "Promise you'll stay safe," Charlie said, unable to hold back the emotion as it threatened to close her throat.

A soft sob came from Hollyn's chest as she tightened her hold on Hollyn. "I will. The bears keep me safe," she said, pulling back to look into her cousin's eyes. "The panthers will keep you safe. My mate trusts them." Hollyn turned a watery gaze to Noah behind the bar. "I trust them. You can trust them, too."

Charlie's eyes immediately found Aron. And he was still watching her closely.

Maybe all that attention from a Shifter should've unnerved her. But it didn't. It made her feel safe. And cared for. Two things she hadn't felt since…

Well, ever. She couldn't remember the last time she'd felt safe. And since her family died when she was young, it had been years since she'd allowed anyone close enough to care about her.

She had somehow subconsciously allowed these people into her life. Shifter or not, when Charlie looked at Aron, all she saw was a man. An incredibly good looking, caring, loyal man.

Hollyn walked Charlie to Aron's truck with Aron following closely behind. The panthers flanked Hollyn and Charlie on either side as if giving her yet one more barrier against the outside world. They were making sure she felt safe.

But as they neared Aron's truck, she realized she hadn't been afraid the whole night. Okay. Maybe she'd been nervous when they had first arrived at Moe's. How could she not when she was in the middle of a room full of Shifters?

Not now. Not since she had realized she still had at least one family member remaining.

She wasn't alone on this planet. She now had Hollyn back. And she'd managed to gain a whole new set of friends.

Hollyn stepped back when Aron opened the door for Charlie and waited for her to say her goodbyes and climb in.

"Do you have a phone?" Hollyn asked.

Charlie pulled hers out and programmed Hollyn's number in, then called her cousin so she'd have Charlie's.

"Call me. Every day," Hollyn said with one more hug.

Charlie noticed how far back Aron stood as Hollyn and Charlie hugged. Their eyes met and a tiny smile ghosted across his lips before he dropped his eyes. He rarely held eye contact more than a few seconds at a time. Except at Moe's.

Raising her hand in a wave, Charlie said goodnight to the people crowded by the front door of the bar and climbed into the seat of Aron's truck. They all waved back, huge grins on their face.

Before tonight, she'd had very little interaction with their kind. Her first real introduction into their world was the night her entire family had been slaughtered. The second was the night she had been kidnapped.

And then the panthers had rushed up that hill and fought by her side, fought to protect her.

Now, she had a mad crush on one and was becoming fast friends with a big group of them.

What an odd night. What an odd twist of events.

Had someone told her a mere two months ago her life would revolve around Shifters she would've laughed in their face.

Not now.

Now…she found herself wanting Aron in her life as more than a bodyguard.

****

Aron aimed his truck for home, his attention split between the road beneath them and the woman sitting beside him.

He had seen the strength in Charlie shine through tonight. He knew it was there. He'd just had no idea taking her out would have been what brought it out.

As much as Aron would like to pretend it was him or even his friends who had helped her, he knew it was the knowledge she still had a part of her family on this planet.

Glancing over at Charlie as one of the few streetlights on the highway passed, Aron spotted the soft smile on her lips as she watched through the windshield. She was happy.

"I can take you back to Moe's tomorrow if you want," Aron offered without a second thought.

He saw Charlie look at him from his periphery. Meeting her gaze for a second, he nodded and smiled. "As much as you want," he promised.

He would do anything to see that smile on her face as often as possible.

Even as the thought crossed his mind it both shocked him and felt right. He couldn't deny to himself that he wanted her. His panther wanted her.

But he knew he couldn't have her.

Or maybe it was that he *shouldn't*. She was a victim they'd assigned themselves to protect.

So was Hollyn, Aron's panther reminded him.

He was a Shifter. Charlie was a Fairy.

Noah's a Shifter. Hollyn is a Fairy.

"Shut up," he whispered to his panther.

"What?" Charlie said, turning to look at him.

"Nothing. Thinking out loud," he lied.

"Thank you for taking me there tonight," Charlie said after a few moments of silence. "I didn't want to go. But…you were right. I needed to get out of the house."

"I don't remember saying that," Aron said, frowning over at her before looking back at the road as they rolled up to a red light. When they were at a full stop, he turned his attention fully to the beautiful woman sitting beside him. "But I'm glad you went."

She nodded and pulled her bottom lip into her mouth to chew on it. And Aron had an overwhelming urge to pull that lip from her teeth and run the pad of his thumb over it.

Instead, he wrapped his fingers around the steering wheel so tight his knuckles turned white.

The light turned green. Aron pushed on the gas a little too hard and saw Charlie's head whip backward out of the corner of his eye.

Easing off the gas pedal, he glanced over at her. "Sorry."

"Did I say something?" she said, her voice soft.

"Nope."

He had no intention of telling her exactly what was wrong. Because he had no intention of doing anything that would make her uncomfortable. And that was one hell of an uncomfortable conversation.

Charlie hadn't turned on her porch light or any lamps inside. The house was bathed in darkness.

Not safe.

"Stay here," he said as he pushed from the truck.

"No way," she said, jumping from the passenger seat and jogging to catch up with his long legs.

When Aron frowned down at her in confusion and question, she shook her head.

"They got me out here. I'm not staying out here by myself."

That pissed Aron off. Badly. There was no reason she should feel unsafe in her own yard. A home was a refuge. It was where one should feel safest. And those assholes had taken that from her.

Charlie slipped her small hand into his and Aron twined his fingers through hers. Her hand was so soft, so warm. And the size reminded him of how fragile and vulnerable she was, even if she had her Elemental gift to call upon.

Tightening his grip, he pulled her behind him as he climbed the porch. "Will you stay here? Please?" he whispered as softly as he could.

Her wide pale eyes were locked on his face as she nodded in jerky movements.

Holding up one finger, he released his hold on her and held his hand out for her keys. Just because it was locked now didn't mean someone hadn't broken in. Every single one of the panthers were adept at lock picking. Someone could've broken in, relocked the door, and laid in wait for her.

Aron slid the key into the door as softly as possible and then opened the door without a sound. Raising his head, he sniffed, trying to detect anyone or anything out of place.

All he smelled was Charlie. Her unique feminine scent. It was a powdery, flowery smell mixed with something earthy.

Pulling it into his lungs, he closed his eyes and savored the sensation rushing through his body. His panther purred in response.

As he opened his eyes and took in his surroundings, he made sure nothing looked out of place. He didn't really know what her house normally looked like as he'd yet to come in here, but he didn't see any overturned furniture or papers strewn everywhere. Instead, he was met with a tidy, girly house.

Creeping from room to room, he checked every shadow, behind every door, even under the bed. When he was sure there was no one there to hurt Charlie, he stepped back outside, making room for her to pass him without touching.

Why? Why was he still insisting on sticking with these stupid rules? He'd held her hand twice tonight. Twice. One of those times, she'd initiated the hand holding.

But Aron was a creature of habit. And rules. And laws. He liked knowing what he could and couldn't do. What he didn't like was not being able to pull Charlie into his arms as she looked into his face with watery eyes.

"Is there someone inside?"

"No," he said, his arms aching with the need to hold her.

"Then why did you make me stay out here?" She blinked rapidly, angrily swiping a tear from her cheek that escaped over lashes.

Was she mad at him now? She was angry that he'd checked her house for any intruders?

"Your house and yard were dark. I wanted to make sure no one was creeping around waiting for you to get home."

Charlie slapped his chest. "I thought they were here for me again, you jerk," she said.

She'd slapped him. She had actually slapped his chest. Of course, there was no strength behind it. But still…she was mad at him.

"I just wanted to make sure you were safe, Charlie. I didn't mean to freak you out."

Charlie's nostrils flared as she inhaled deeply and blew it out as another tear fell over her lashes.

Aron couldn't stop himself. He reached forward and wiped it away with the tip of his finger.

"I'm sorry," he said.

She nodded and took another deep breath. "I know. I'm sorry, too. I didn't mean to hit you." Her eyes dropped to his chest before raising again. "Did I hurt you?"

Aron snorted out a laugh. "No. You didn't hurt me."

Charlie scrubbed her face with both hands. "You want to come in?"

Opening his mouth to say no, Aron changed his mind. She had invited him in on several occasions over the past few weeks and he always declined the invitation. Not tonight. Tonight, he wanted to be near her. He wanted to make sure he hadn't pushed her too far by taking her to Moe's. He wanted…

Hell, he just wanted to be with her.

"Yeah. I'll come in."

The surprise that came over her face almost made Aron bust out laughing. But he didn't want her to think he was laughing at her.

"It's a mess," she said as she stepped in ahead of him.

"No, it's not. I already saw it, remember," he said, following her in.

Charlie turned on the lamp beside the couch and pulled her sweater off her shoulders, hanging it on the back of the chair pushed up to the kitchen table. It was a small place, but not cramped. The furniture was a little small for someone his size.

"You hungry or thirsty? I have some beer."

"A beer is fine," he said, really taking in the room now that he wasn't looking for a threat.

There were no personal photos anywhere but there was quite a bit of artwork on the walls. The couch was floral but not pastel. There was a darker rug beneath the antique looking coffee table, but the short couch was modern and sturdy. It was a mixture of designs yet it all flowed perfectly.

It was as if her house was a reflection of Charlie – a mix of femininity and softness with strength and aged wisdom. How old was Charlie? He knew the Fae tended to live longer than other species, but they weren't immortal.

They still grew old and died.

They could still be killed.

Charlie carried two beers to the couch and sat, setting one of the bottles on a coaster sitting on the coffee table.

After a few minutes, Charlie looked up at Aron. "You can sit."

The couch was so small. It was going to be damned near impossible to refrain from touching her.

Even though that was all he wanted to do.

Lowering onto the small piece of furniture, Aron reached for his beer, taking it to his lips for a long pull.

"Why don't you touch me?" she blurted out, and almost caused Aron to choke.

"What?" he said after swallowing.

"Tonight was the first time you've ever touched me. And that was only because I was scared. Both times we held hands it was only because I was scared." She chewed on the inside of her cheek for a second. "Do you not like me? I mean, are you annoyed you have to babysit me?"

Aron set his beer down. "One – we're not babysitting you. We want to make sure you're safe and getting your life back. We do that with every woman we rescue when we can."

A brief look of disappointment flashed through her pretty eyes.

"And two, I like you." In more ways than one. But he'd keep that to himself.

"So then why don't you touch me? Why do all of you avoid even looking at me? It's like I'm this…thing you're responsible for and you all begrudge me for it."

Well, shit. This was another conversation he hadn't really wanted to get into. How the hell could he explain all of this to her?

"It's out of respect," he said after trying to find the right words.

Her light blonde brows lowered and her eyes narrowed. "You guys won't look at me or hug me or even touch me…out of respect." Her tone was incredulous.

Aron ran his fingers through his hair and searched the room for a better explanation. Of course, nothing in her house gave him the answers. It only made him want to ask her about each and every piece of furniture and art in her home. He wanted to know everything about her. But he couldn't do that without spending more time with her.

How the hell could he explain this shit to her?

"Okay. Have you noticed how the panthers rarely talk to any of the mated females?"

She nodded, her brows still pulled low.

"It's out of respect for both the female and the mating bond."

"How is ignoring a woman showing respect?"

Charlie sounded so much like Campbell at that moment. Brax's mate had hated the way the panthers interacted with her and other women and had done everything in her power to break their long-held ways. She constantly bumped them with her shoulder or made sure she was close enough when they moved by her that they would have to touch her when they passed.

"We're not ignoring you. Or other women." Damn it. He was screwing this up. "Panthers see it as flirting."

"Talking to a woman isn't the same thing as flirting," Charlie said, pulling her legs up and tucking them beneath her. Her knee brushed his leg and caused his panther to purr again.

"I know that. It's just…damn it," he said aloud. "We don't want to make a woman feel uncomfortable. We don't want anyone to feel as if we're pressuring them into anything. We feel as if women are…well, royalty. You're a queen. Without females, all living creatures cease to exist. We don't interact much with mated females because we don't want to disrespect the bond or cause the male to grow possessive."

"So then why do the rest of the Pride avoid me like the plague? I'm not mated."

Charlie watched him closely. Her brows dropped lower then raised to her hairline. "I'm not mated, am I?"

"You'd know if you were," Aron said, and couldn't keep the growl of his panther out of his voice.

Her eyes narrowed. "Aron?"

"Yeah?"

"Am I your mate?"

Aron's heart tripled its pace and his mouth went dry. How the fuck was he supposed to answer that? Yeah. She was his mate. Or at least he and his animal both wanted her to be their mate. But she had a choice. All females had a choice. It didn't matter what he wanted. It mattered what she wanted.

And he realized he hadn't turned his eyes from her face the entire time they'd been talking.

"Is that why the Pride avoids me? Do they think I'm your mate?" Her voice was barely above a whisper as her gaze dropped to his lips then raised back up to his eyes.

She wanted honesty. He could see it all over her face.

He was terrified, though. Terrified to admit it, and terrified it would scare her away.

If she told him to leave, he would. He'd make sure the other members of Ravenwood would keep her safe and give her the distance she needed.

Or, she could accept him.

Fuck. He wanted her to accept him so bad. *Needed* her to accept him.

"Yes."

"Yes to which question?" she asked. She was leaning forward a little now.

"Yes, they avoid you because they think you're my mate. And yes…I want you as my mate." She blinked a few times then pulled her bottom lip between her teeth again. "But you have a choice, Charlie. I would never force you to do any—"

His words were cut off by her lips as she quickly closed the space between them and kissed him. It was a soft kiss, her full lips tentative at first.

When he raised his hand to cup the back of her head, she sighed. Aron tilted his head and deepened the kiss, moaning when she opened for him and teased his tongue with hers.

After a few minutes of the most amazing kiss of his life, Charlie pulled back, her eyes now a brighter blue as they widened at him. "I knew it," she whispered.

"How?"

Shaking her head, she pulled away but kept her body leaned toward Aron. "I don't know. I just…did. I mean, not right away. I thought it was me. That I had a major crush on you. But my magic has been pulling toward you since that first day in the woods. I thought at the time it wanted me to protect you. But it hasn't stopped."

Holy shit. Her magic had claimed him the same way his panther had claimed her. And by that kiss, he knew she wanted him. She fucking wanted him.

She'd accepted him. She'd accepted the fact he believed her to be his mate.

And now, an entirely new fear nearly stopped his heart.

He had to keep her safe. He would lay down his own life to keep her safe. He would rip his heart from his chest to keep his mate, his beautiful Fairy, out of the hands of the enemy.

Chapter Three

Charlie's heart was beating a mile a minute and she was having a hard time getting air into her lungs.

She'd known. She had known something was different about Aron, about the way she felt about him.

Her magic had been pulling her toward him for weeks now. But she'd constantly tried to chalk it up to a mere crush. No way could her magic have a crush, though.

The second their lips touched she knew it was right. She knew nothing could ever hurt her as long as Aron was in her life. And she knew to the bottom of her soul she'd protect him as much as he'd protect her.

She wasn't some tiny damsel in distress. She had her wind, damn it. Just because those Shifters had caught her off guard didn't mean she would allow it to happen again.

It had taken Aron to help her remember herself. It had taken his friends to remind her of the strength she carried. She might not have been fully mentally healed from her ordeal, but she now had something to fight for. She needed to be the woman he believed her to be, the woman she was before that night.

"So, what does this all mean?" Charlie asked. Fae didn't marry or mate. They formed a blood bond. Something she couldn't do with Aron. And he couldn't mark her as his or she could be killed. One bite could poison her system.

"It means I'll dote on you for the rest of your life." That ghost of a smile was on his lips again.

Had she seen him smile yet? She tried to remember every single interaction and couldn't remember a single time that he had grinned or even smiled.

Then and there she decided she would make it her life's mission to pull as many smiles from him as she could.

"Will you stay tonight?" she blurted before she had a chance to think about it.

Aron's brows shot up to this hairline and a crooked grin pulled one side of his mouth up.

She had just wondered if she'd ever seen him smile. And there it was.

"I mean to sleep. Will you *sleep* here tonight?" she said, backpedaling as fast as she could. "You can have my bed and I'll take the couch if you don't want to sleep with me. No, that's not what I meant. Oh my gosh," she muttered, covering her eyes with her hand.

Fingers gently wrapped around her wrist and pulled her hand away. A breathtaking smile was plastered on Aron's face and his body shook lightly with a laugh he was trying to hold in.

All she'd had to do to make him smile was make a fool of herself? Oh, come *on*!

"I knew what you meant," he said.

"You should smile more," she said, reaching forward and touching his cheek. The stubble tickled her palm as he nuzzled against her hand.

The quiet guy she'd thought about for the past six weeks turned out to be a sweet and affectionate man. And boy could he kiss.

"I'll take the couch. You need your rest," he said after a few minutes of staring at each other.

Even in those moments, it wasn't awkward. It was as if they were searching each other's souls. Seeing through the other straight into the core of their being.

Charlie might not know Aron as well as she would like, but she was already willing to put everything she was on the line to keep him safe and in her life.

She was unsure of what to do or say next. Half lie. She totally wanted to throw her leg over his lap and straddle him.

Charlie excused herself to get ready for bed. After a quick shower, she brushed her teeth, braided her hair back, and then pulled the door open only wide enough to peek her head around the corner before running to her room to get dressed. Charlie pulled on a tank top and a pair of sweatpants, then shoved her feet into some warm, fuzzy socks.

Aron sat exactly where she'd left him and was sitting in the exact same position. Just like earlier when she'd left him outside while she had run in to change before they headed for Moe's.

His eyes raised from his phone, lowered, then shot back up. His gaze roamed her from head to toe before focusing on her face again. There was a slight green glow behind his irises. It was beautiful.

"What?" she said, crossing her arms over her chest as the extra attention made her nervous.

"You're beautiful," he muttered so softly she barely heard it.

"Thank you."

Where earlier, the silence didn't bother her, now it was deafening. Neither of them spoke, and Charlie found it hard to look at him as he continued to stare at her. He had gone from barely glancing at her from time to time to leaving his eyes glued to her.

"Am I making you uncomfortable?"

Charlie couldn't help shuffling her feet. "A little."

The couch creaked under Aron's weight as he pushed to his feet. Charlie looked up at him and frowned as he moved to the front door. "Where are you going? I thought you said you'd stay here tonight?"

"I never want you to feel uncomfortable or like I'm forcing you to do anything, Charlie. I'll sleep on the porch. You'll know I'm here and you're safe so you can sleep, but you won't have to worry about me doing anything you don't want me to do."

"No. It's not that. I know you would never do anything to hurt me."

"Then what?"

"I know I'm not beautiful, Aron," she said, wishing she could suck the words back into her mouth the second they left. "I'm way too skinny. I don't have big boobs like the other women you're friends with. I don't have the curves or whatever anymore. Not that I had a whole lot to begin with. I know you're trying to be nice and I appreciate it, but...yeah. You keep staring at me and I'm imagining you cataloguing every single flaw."

Aron's head snapped back as if Charlie had struck him. "Flaws?"

Charlie dropped her eyes to her feet.

"Yeah. You're a little on the thin side. You've also been through a trauma that would send most women to a psychiatric facility. Not you." He took a step closer. "You ran back up that hill to fight even after Campbell got you to safety." Another step closer. "You didn't run away. You didn't move out of town. You lied every single time anyone asked if you were okay." Another step. "You showed strength before you remembered how strong you really are."

Aron was now within touching distance. Charlie tilted her head back to look up into his face. His hand raised and cupped her cheek and Charlie nuzzled against his hand the same way he'd done hers less than a half an hour ago.

"When I said you're beautiful, I meant it. You are the most beautiful woman I've ever seen. Inside and out. If you think you're too thin, I'll simply have to take you to Moe's more to fatten you up."

And there was that sweet, crooked smile again.

"You'll stay in here tonight?" she asked, wrapping her arms around his waist.

When had she become so brazen? They had literally only admitted to each other tonight, less than an hour ago, that they had feelings beyond friendship. Yet, she found it hard to keep herself from touching him now.

"I'll stay in here tonight," he said, wrapping his arms around her shoulders and pulling her against his chest.

Charlie could stay like that all night, simply listening to his heart thud behind his ribs. It was soothing. Aron began to sway, and it felt like they were dancing to music only they could hear.

It was perfect.

After what felt like an eternity, yet not nearly enough time, Aron pulled back. "You need to get some sleep. Do you have to be anywhere in the morning? Do you need me to wake you up at any certain time?"

Charlie shook her head. She had been living off money her parents had left her when they died. If she was careful, she wouldn't need to get a job anytime in the near future.

"Good. Sleep. I'm out here. I won't let anyone get anywhere near you. I'll hear or scent them if they even step on your property. Remember that. You are absolutely safe tonight."

Smiling up at him, she tilted her face to him, wrapped a hand around the back of his neck, and pulled him down for one more kiss. She had a feeling she'd never get tired of kissing Aron.

****

Sunlight shone behind Charlie's closed lids. Pulling her arms over her head, she stretched and smiled. She hadn't woken up from a single nightmare before the sun rose. How strange.

And then she remembered Aron said he would stay the night. Had he? Was he still here? What time was it?

Picking up her phone from her nightstand, she brought the screen to life and looked wide-eyed at the digital numbers switching from eleven thirty-three to eleven thirty-four. She'd slept until almost noon. She couldn't remember the last time she'd slept that late.

Charlie threw her legs over the side of the bed and padded quietly to her bedroom door she'd left cracked open last night. Pulling it open and wincing when the hinges squeaked, she peeked her head around the corner.

Aron was asleep on the floor right outside her room. He'd opted to sleep on the floor rather than the sofa. Why? To make her feel safer?

She stood there staring down at his softly snoring body and tried to decide whether she should creep back to her bed and wait for him to wake up, wake him up and offer him breakfast, or simply step over him. She did have to use the restroom and his big body stood right smack in the middle of the space separating her room and the bathroom.

He looked so peaceful, though. She would hate to have to pull him out of whatever dream left that soft smile on his full lips.

Was he dreaming about her? Was it a sexy dream? She would be a liar if she said she'd never dreamed about him naked, all his delicious weight pressing her down into her mattress.

Even as she stood there wondering, she realized something had changed inside of her. She wasn't sure if it was the fact she realized she was no longer alone on this planet or the fact Aron made her feel safe in her own home again. Whichever was the case, it felt awesome.

That simple thought helped her make up her mind. She wanted him awake. She wanted him off the floor. And she wanted to cook for him. It was the least she could do.

Well, shoot. What all did she have in her fridge? She hadn't had much of an appetite for so long and had been so terrified to leave to go to the grocery store. She knew she had eggs and bread. Maybe even some milk. She could make him something her mom used to make her on cold, winter mornings – toast and gravy with eggs. Wasn't exactly biscuits and gravy, but it was better than nothing. And she had always loved it.

Lowering to her knees, Charlie lightly laid a hand on Aron's shoulder. "Aron," she whispered, shaking him gently. "Wake up. It's time for breakfast."

Aron's eyes fluttered, but never fully opened. He wrapped his fingers around Charlie's wrist and pulled her down until she was resting on his chest.

With a giggle, she tried to pull away. "Aron," she said a little louder this time. "Wake up."

Did he realize who she was? Did he realize he had not only pulled her onto his own body but had a pretty impressive erection tenting his jeans?

Aron's eyes opened to slits and he smiled at her groggily. "What time is it?" he asked, his voice hoarse with sleep.

"Almost noon," she said, not quite ready to fully pull away from him. She could feel his heat through her sweatpants and his hand was still wrapped softly around her wrist.

Aron lifted his head and looked around the room. He looked disoriented when he turned narrowed eyes to Charlie. "I slept until noon?"

Charlie shrugged up her shoulders. "We were up kind of late." She moved back when Aron sat up. "You hungry? I want to make you breakfast."

"You don't have to do that," he said as he scrubbed both hands up and down his face like he was trying to scrub away the sleepiness.

"I want to. It's the least I can do."

When Charlie started to climb to her feet, Aron stopped her with a hand on her arm like he'd done when she woke him. "You don't owe me anything, Charlie."

"I owe you everything, Aron. I owe your Pride everything. You guys saved my life. You kept me from being sold off or poisoned. You helped me find myself again. You gave me back my family."

His thumb caressed the side of her arm as he kept his hand clasped onto her. "You were fighting back before we got there. You found your own strength. None of us had anything to do with that. And as much as I'd love to take credit for giving you Hollyn, I had no idea you were family."

Charlie lowered back to her butt so she could look into Aron's face. "You saved Hollyn. Like you did me. You kept her alive. If you hadn't done that, I wouldn't have her in my life."

Aron pressed his palm against her cheek. "I would do anything as long as it kept you safe and made you happy.

****

Aron wanted to continue to argue with her, to tell her he had nothing to do with her newfound strength. Not newfound. *Rediscovered.*

Yeah. He'd taken her to Moe's to get some real food in her, but she had been the one to pull from herself. She'd been the one to square her shoulders and meet a room full of Shifters head on.

Memories of the night before slowly came back as Charlie pushed to her feet and headed for the kitchen. He'd admitted she was his mate. Actually, she'd guessed it. He just hadn't denied it. And she'd accepted the bond. He could never mark her as his own, but she'd agreed to the pairing. She had admitted she felt as strongly for him as he did for her.

Still, he wouldn't be the one to make any first moves. Couldn't. She'd kissed him first. Anything after that would have to be on her timeline.

Charlie leaned forward and pressed a quick kiss to Aron's lips as if they'd kissed good morning a thousand times then stood quickly and stepped over him.

Aron watched her hips sway as she hurried into the kitchen and started rummaging through her fridge and cabinets. He had no idea what she was going to make or even if she was a good cook, but it didn't matter. It was something she wanted to do for him, a way to show him her gratitude even if it wasn't needed.

"You mind if I use your shower?" Aron asked as he pushed to a sitting position.

"Help yourself. Towels are in the closet behind the door." She smiled at him and Aron felt his heart flutter the same time his panther purred. And he suddenly felt like an idiot even thinking the word flutter.

More and more, he was beginning to understand his friends' need to constantly touch their mates. The short time it took him to shower, dress in the clothes he'd slept in, then finger brush his teeth was enough to make his human and animal side antsy.

"Smells good," he said as he exited the hallway and stepped into the living room that connected to the kitchen.

"Hope it tastes good, too," she said as she heaped food on both plates and set them on the table.

"You hungry?" he teased then wished he could suck the words back into his mouth.

The last thing Charlie needed was to be reminded of her lack of appetite.

But she didn't look phased by his comment. She simply smiled and winked as she lowered into her seat catty corner to Aron's.

"I'm starving. I've always had a huge appetite and after going so long without eating…guess it caught up with me."

She dove into her food, her eyes rolling shut as she chewed.

And fuck if Aron couldn't stop the thought of whether she'd look like that during orgasm.

Before he made himself look like an asshole and say or do something that would make Charlie uncomfortable, Aron lowered his eyes to his plate and focused on eating. She'd made eggs and bacon with some buttered toast on the side. And yeah, it was damn good. From the taste of the sunny side up eggs, she'd used the bacon grease to fry them.

His mate was a country girl, even if she hadn't grown up here her whole life.

"Where'd you learn to cook?" Aron asked after swallowing.

Charlie held up one finger as she chewed, then took a drink of her coffee. "This isn't really cooking," she said with another of those sexy winks. "But I learned by watching videos on YouTube. And TV. I love those cooking shows. I might not be able to make half of what they do, but I love watching and pretending someday I'll make a braised duck or something fancy like that."

There she was. He was seeing the real Charlie, not the broken Charlie. And his heart swelled more than he thought possible.

Even when she was terrified of her own shadow, Aron had seen her strength. And all it had taken was seeing her cousin to help her find it again.

"Do you have plans today?" Aron asked before taking a bite of the toast.

She shook her head. "Nope. Until last night, I hadn't thought about leaving my house ever again. Not true. I thought about moving away, far away from here."

The swelling of Aron's heart was gone. Now, it was barely beating. If she needed to leave, he wouldn't stop her. But the thought of her no longer in his life made his stomach turn.

"You want to move?"

She shrugged up one shoulder. "Not really. Not anymore. Especially not since Hollyn lives here…and since I have you."

Aron's face split into a wide grin. He released the breath he hadn't realized he'd been holding in a rush of air.

"What? Did you think I'd leave you?" She smiled a wry smile at him. "Would you miss me?" She batted her eye lashes.

Schooling his face into an emotionless mask, he did like she had done and shrugged up one shoulder. "Nah. I'm sure I could find someone else to make me eggs and bacon."

Charlie slapped his shoulder. "Hey!"

He chuckled and shook his head. "If you left, I…I don't know what I'd do, to be honest. I wouldn't stop you. I would never keep you from doing anything. Or make you do anything. But it would break my heart."

Charlie watched Aron, not saying a word. But the emotions were all over her face. He had overwhelmed her. He had to be more careful of blurting shit out like that in the future.

After a few awkward moments of silence, she cleared her throat. "So, why did you ask if I had any plans today?"

"My friends have cookouts every weekend. They barbecue and drink beer around a fire pit. It's a good time."

"It's chilly today."

"Not really. At least not to us. And there will be a fire pit."

Tilting her head to one side, she chewed on the inside of her cheek. "Will it be the same people from last night?"

"Yep. And a few you didn't get to meet. Colton and Shawnee weren't there."

"Shawnee's the pregnant female?" Charlie asked.

"Yeah. She's carrying twins. Or possibly more. They're not sure since they can't exactly go to the hospital for an ultrasound and bloodwork. She doesn't get out much. She still might not be able to make it if she isn't feeling well."

"Twins?" Charlie said. She looked so sweet and wistful. "She's having twins?"

"Or more. Shawnee's a lioness."

Her pale brows pinched tighter. "I thought you said they were part of the bear Clan."

"They are. But Shawnee came from a different Pride. It's a long story and not mine to tell."

If he wasn't mistaken, Aron could've sworn he saw respect in Charlie's eyes, and she nodded her head.

"What time is this cookout?"

Charlie stood and started clearing the table.

"Let me do that. You cooked."

"You can help me," she said as she turned on the faucet and grabbed a sponge.

Aron sidled beside Charlie and took the dishes to dry as she washed and rinsed them. "Usually around two or so. I'll text one of the wolves and find out."

He watched her out of the corner of his eye and waited for her to tense at the mention of wolves. But she didn't. That soft smile that had appeared at the mention of Shawnee's pregnancy was still there.

"Are you okay with hanging out with Shifters all day?"

"I've met most of them. They were really nice to me." She took the dish towel from him and laid it over the edge of the sink. "Will Hollyn be there?"

"I'm not sure. She works the bar with Noah most days. I'll text him and ask if he'll let her off work."

"I don't want to put everyone out. I'm just kind of excited about being among the living again."

He couldn't help the surprised laugh that burst from his mouth. "You're excited about going out?"

A pink hue washed over her cheeks. "Okay. I'm a little nervous. But I have to pull myself out of this or I'm going to make myself crazy. I like your friends. They're nice. I can't see any of them stealing women or selling them to psychos."

"Hell no. They fought against people like that. They fought alongside my Pride to make sure female Shifters had a choice about their own lives."

"Yeah. I know about that. I'm...I don't know. I want to be normal again, but I still get so scared. Last night was the first night I've slept without nightmares in six weeks. And you'll have to go home tonight."

"Why would I have to go home?" Aron asked, leaning against the counter and crossing his arms over his chest.

"Don't you have a job? A house of your own?"

"Well, yeah. But I can bring a change of clothes over and sleep right there on the floor again if it'll help you sleep. And my house is shared with the rest of the Pride."

"Campbell lives with you guys?"

"Nah. Her and Brax stay at her place most nights. They only stay at the trailer when we hunt for rogues late into the night."

"Would you have hunted for rogues last night if I hadn't asked you to stay the night?"

She chewed on her bottom lip as she waited for him to answer.

He did *not* want to tell her the truth. He could already see a little guilt coming into her eyes at the thought of another woman being stolen away when the panthers could've possibly stopped it. But there were only the five of them and a shit ton of bad guys in the world.

"I'm sure the rest of the Pride and Campbell still hunted."

"Campbell isn't part of your Pride? Is it because she's human?"

"She is a part of the Pride. But…well, for one thing, none of us want her to hunt with us. It's too dangerous."

"Because she's a woman? I'm pretty sure I saw her kicking butt when you guys came rushing into the woods."

"Not because she's a woman. I know a lot of females who could kick my ass. It's because she's not a Shifter. She's fragile. One well-placed scratch or bite could Turn her. And there's no guarantee she'd survive her first Shift. Or she could be killed. Easily. But she was doing it before we met her. I would never force her into anything."

"You've said that before."

"Said what before?" Aron asked.

"You said before I had a choice, that you would never force anything on me."

He dipped his chin once.

"Why do you keep saying that?" Charlie asked, moving from the kitchen and lowering onto the couch. When she pulled her feet under her, she looked even smaller.

"That's the way of my people. Women are royalty. Period. You control everything I do and say. You control everything I am. I told you earlier if you decided to move, I'd let you go without a single argument, even if it ripped my heart from my chest and caused my panther to go insane. I mean that with anything and everything."

"I kissed you," she said, but it sounded more as if she were thinking aloud rather than saying something to him. "You didn't kiss me, I kissed you. Both times." She'd looked off to the side as if thinking. When she returned her eyes to his face, the pale blue had morphed into a darker color. The change was barely there, but it was there.

Aron waited for her to work the new information through her head. He hoped it wouldn't be the thing that scared her away. But why would it? He'd basically told her she held his entire world in her thin hand.

Maybe it was too much. Too intense.

"You didn't kiss me. You waited for me to make the first move," she said, looking at him fully, her eyes narrowed. "You'll wait for me to make every first move, won't you?"

He dipped his chin again and waited.

A smile slowly stretched across her beautiful lips. "That's kind of romantic. On the other hand, it kind of makes me feel powerful."

"It doesn't freak you out?"

"Why would it?"

Aron crossed the room and sat beside her, taking her hand in his. "I thought it would be too intense or overwhelming."

"Aron, you just told me I'm your entire world. You just told me...well, you told me you love me in your own way." Her lips snapped shut and her eyes went wide. "Or did I hear what I wanted to hear?" she asked barely above a whisper.

"Do *you* love *me*?" he asked. Yep. That was what he was clinging to, because why else would she have brought it up?

"I asked you first."

And, suddenly, he felt like a teenager on one of those drama shows.

He really didn't know how he felt. He knew he didn't want to live life without Charlie. He knew that he fought himself daily against rushing to her house to make sure she was safe. He knew that her face was the last think he thought about every night before going to sleep.

And he knew he wanted that beautiful smile to make a reappearance on her face. Now.

"I do love you. And I'm probably going to screw things up. A lot. I've never loved a woman other than my mom. Well, and my friends. But I've never loved like this."

"Me neither," she said, then dipped her head with an embarrassed smile. "I mean, I've never loved a man like this."

"You do love me?"

"Well, yeah," she said, her brows dipping slightly as if the answer should've been obvious.

And then they sat there staring at each other. Aron wasn't sure what to do next. He'd let her make the first moves, but all he knew was he could never mark her, could never leave his scent permanently embedded in her blood for any Shifter in the area to know she was off limits.

Chapter Four

Charlie watched as trees passed. She could do this. She'd hung out with all of them last night. And there would be no extra strangers around. Only people Aron trusted.

"Do they all know I'm a Fairy?" she asked, turning to look at his profile.

He looked so yummy. A dark pair of sunglasses hid his beautiful eyes, a little scruff shadowed his cheeks and jaw from not shaving last night, and his jeans were worn and hugged his strong legs perfectly.

He rested his wrist along the top of the steering wheel and was the epitome of cool and relaxed.

"I don't think so. Noah knows Hollyn is Fae because she's his mate. So, I assume he knows you are, too. It's your secret to tell. But I promise you, the people we're hanging out with today I would trust them with my life. If I had any sisters, I would've been honored for them to be mated to any single one of the males."

"And the females?"

Aron chuckled. "I feel like I need to warn you about a few people, but not in a bad way," Aron said, scratching at his stubble as they rolled to a stop light.

"But you'd trust them?"

"Absolutely."

"So then what do you want to warn me about?"

She'd expected a wave of anxiety and fear to hit her, but it didn't. She wasn't sure how much of it was Aron's presence and how much of it was her own strength.

Or maybe it was a combination of both.

"Do you remember meeting Nova?" he asked, glancing over at her once as he pulled away from the light.

"There were a lot of people."

"True," he said. "Nova is the mate of Gray. Gray is the Alpha of the Big River Pack."

"Okay."

"She's a trip. So is Emory. And Reed. They'll have you cracking up the whole night. But Nova is…kind of a perv."

He smiled as he shook his head so, obviously, he meant perv in an affectionate manner.

"She writes romance books. So, she's always trying to get everyone to tell her about their sex lives. She'll no doubt ask you if we've...done anything," he said.

"She's going to ask if we've had sex?" Charlie asked, her eyes going wide as a nervous giggle worked up her chest.

"Yep. And Emory loves to tease. So does Reed. The two of them have been real close for years."

"Are they mates?"

Aron barked out a laugh. "Hell no. They're more like brother and sister. They both have mates. They'll all be there."

Charlie looked down at herself then over at Aron. She was dressed in a similar manner, but where he wore a t-shirt, she was layered with a t-shirt under a flannel and topped off with a hoodie.

"You sure I look okay?" she asked.

"You're beautiful. Everyone already likes you. After they spend more time with you, they'll love you."

He sounded so confident Charlie believed him. "Did you find out whether Hollyn would be there or not?"

"Noah said she's going to try to get off early. But since it's the weekend, they tend to get busy and are shorthanded with Shawnee on maternity leave." He got quiet for a second. After he flipped his signal on to turn down a long, dirt road, Aron glanced at her. "You think you'll tell them you're a Fairy?"

Charlie shrugged. She'd thought about that. But there was really no reason to divulge that part of herself unless the subject came up. What was she supposed to say? *Hey guys! Great to meet you. I'm a Fairy and can conjure a tornado with magic.*

Nope. She'd keep it to herself until the moment arrived when she had no choice but to spill her guts.

"Um. Before we get there, I wanted to talk to you about something," she said, then immediately pulled her bottom lip between her teeth to worry it.

Aron was a good guy. She knew no matter what she said, he'd never yell at her or hurt her. But she also knew he was super protective of not only her, but all females. It was ingrained in his very being.

"What's up?" he asked with a worried frown.

"I was thinking about what we were talking about earlier, about Campbell hunting with you guys," she said as she glanced at him from the corner of her eye.

Even if she hadn't looked at him, she would've felt the anger and fear rolling from him a mile away. He'd stopped the car on the dirt road and was staring at her as if she'd grown two heads.

"I really hope this conversation isn't going where I think it is." He rubbed his forehead like the mere thought of her trailing along with them was giving him a headache.

"Hear me out," she said.

Really, she couldn't believe she was thinking it, let alone about to say it out loud. But she knew Aron would have a hard time being away from her. And she slept so much better when he was at her house. *And* she wanted to help eradicate the traffickers.

It might take her a while to be as brave as Campbell and the panthers, but she could do it. She had her wind and her magic. She'd be their back up.

"I'm not weak."

"I never said you were," he said with raised brows.

"No. I know that. What I mean is I'm not weak and I want to help. Campbell is tough and all, but she's human. You guys can teach me how to fight. And I have my magic. You saw it. And that was after a pretty decent head wound."

Aron's face grew red. No. It was closer to crimson. A vein bulged on his forehead and a muscle ticked in his jaw.

"Remember when I said I'd never try to control your actions. This is one of those times where I'm going to struggle with that."

To Charlie's surprise, his voice was calm and controlled. It didn't match his physical appearance at all.

"You're okay with it? You'll let me hunt with you guys?"

"No. I'm not okay with. At all. But...fuck." The curse was muttered under his breath, then he shot her an apologetic look. "Sorry."

"I won't get in the way. And I won't try to be a hero and go without you guys. I'm not as brave as Campbell," she said as she dipped her eyes.

She'd never thought of herself as a coward, but she would never be courageous enough to rush into the woods alone to take on Shifters.

"You're brave." He went back to rubbing his forehead, then jerked his eyes up as if he'd heard something. "Can we talk about this later?"

Charlie looked in the direction where he'd looked and tensed. "Is someone coming?"

Aron turned his head and smiled reassuringly. "They're yelling at me to hurry up and get you there."

"Oh." They were excited to see her again? She hadn't talked to them that much. She'd been too distracted by the reappearance of a family member.

"We *will* talk about it later," he said as he put the truck into drive and crept forward.

Charlie nodded, but her mind was on the group of people who came into the view as he cleared the long stretch of trees.

"That's a lot of people," she said.

Aron's eyes bounced across the different faces. "Looks like the lionesses from the top of the hill are here, too."

"What lionesses?" she asked. Her voice sounded a little loud and high in her own ears. She could only imagine how it sounded to his super sensitive ones.

Aron parked beside a row of trucks and cars and turned off the engine. His hand dwarfed hers as he took it and squeezed it gently.

"Take a breath. You've met almost everyone here. The lionesses were saved from a piece of shit Pride. They live on the hill. They're a little broken and skittish. They won't talk to you much, but they're safe. I promise. Everyone here is safe."

They were safe. *She* was safe.

"It's about time," a woman said as Aron rounded the front of the truck and let Charlie out.

He took her hand and led her to the group of waiting females.

"I'm Nova. I didn't know if you remembered my name," Nova said as she rushed forward and wrapped her arms around Charlie's shoulders.

"Oh!" Charlie said, using her free arm to wrap it around Nova's back.

Nova pulled back. "You met Emory, Callie, and Peyton at Moe's. Shawnee is the preggo over there," she said, pointing to a very obviously pregnant woman sitting in a chair with her feet propped on a cooler. When she spotted Charlie looking at her, she raised a hand

and waved with a wide smile. "The one with the pink hair and little girl on her hip is Lola. The other females are the lionesses from the Hope Pride. And you met most of the guys except my mate, Gray, Emory's mate, Eli, and, and Preggo's mate, Colton."

She hooked an arm through the crook of Charlie's elbow and started pulling her forward then stopped. "You going to hold on to her all night?" Nova asked Aron.

Aron averted his eyes, nodded once, then released his hold on Charlie.

Nova sighed theatrically. "Still not talking to me? I thought that would change when you got a mate."

His eyes jerked to Nova's face. "How did you…?"

"Oh please," Emory said with a roll of her eyes. "We figured this was coming. We've heard all about your need to camp outside of Charlie's house over the past few weeks."

He'd been camping outside of her house? Charlie turned questioning eyes to Aron.

"It was only a few times." He looked so cute, like a little boy caught in a lie.

Charlie smiled at him and winked.

Emory looped her arm through Charlie's other arm and guided her toward a large circle of lawn chairs around a fire pit.

As they walked, the women chattered on about how they'd only started doing these cookouts a few years ago, about how Callie had crashed into their last fire pit, about the two babies living in the Pack.

The men stood around with beers in their hands, their eyes glued to their mates as they neared. There were so many people. Charlie knew there was no way she'd remember everyone's names tonight. But she'd try. They were all so kind. So welcoming.

Already she felt like she belonged right there among this large family of Shifters. There were so many different kinds of species. Nova and Emory had taken turns naming off every single kind, including Peyton, who'd had a wolf forced into her when she was human. They'd told her how she'd almost died during her first Shift.

"Her animal is insane," Callie whispered.

"I can hear you," Peyton said. But it was obvious to Charlie they were teasing each other.

Had she ever had this? Had she ever had a group of friends this large? She couldn't remember having a friend who wasn't related, let alone a group of friends.

Within the first thirty minutes, Charlie was sitting beside Aron with Nova on her right. She felt like she'd found her home.

And she couldn't help but wonder how much of that feeling had to do with the man brushing his thumb across the back of her hand he was holding.

****

Charlie was amazing. Aron watched in awe as she won over every single person in the Big River Pack, the Blackwater Clan; even the lionesses from the Hope Pride seemed to relax with her there.

He had no idea if it was her magic that drew people in or simply her personality. Whatever it was, he knew exactly how each person felt as they hung on to her every word as though it were the gospel.

"Where are you from?" Micah asked, his bright blue eyes glued to her face.

Everyone loved her but Micah. As usual, the Second in the Pack was leery of the newcomer. He saw everyone as a threat to his mate and Pack. He was loyal and protective of his people.

Aron could respect that. Normally. Right now, it was irritating his panther.

"Micah," Callie said softly and touched his forearm.

"What? I'm just asking a question."

"I'm from all over," Charlie answered.

Micah narrowed her eyes. "A nomad?"

"Not really. I just…I moved around a lot."

"Why?" Micah asked.

"Enough," Aron said, cutting this shit off before it went any further.

If Micah kept pushing her, Charlie would have no choice but to tell the truth about her heritage. And he wouldn't have anyone strong arming her.

"If she doesn't have anything to hide, why not let her answer?" Micah said.

Next to Micah, Aron saw Callie's nostrils flare. She scented the rush of fur in the air. Even from where Aron sat, he could smell

Micah's wolf pushing to get out. Aron's panther was doing the same. He'd never fought one of his friends and he didn't want to start tonight. And he did *not* want to fight in front of Charlie. She'd been through enough to last her a lifetime.

"Leave her the fuck alone," he said.

Micah slowly pushed to his feet. "What the fuck are you two hiding? Are there people after her? Are you bringing danger to our territory? We have fucking cubs here."

Aron released his hold on Charlie's hand and stood, as well.

"If you guys are going to fight, could you go into the field so you don't break shit?" Reed asked.

"Aron?" Charlie's sweet voice broke through the anger simmering deep inside of him.

Her soft hand landed on his forearm and Aron glanced down at her. Her pale eyes were almost as dark as Hollyn's as they stared wide-eyed into his face.

"Let's just go." There was a plea in her words.

"No way. You two aren't going anywhere. Micah, sit down and calm your pits. She hasn't done anything to warrant your crappy attitude," Emory said, leaning forward to see him past her large mate.

"Bull shit. What are you hiding?" Micah asked Charlie.

He wasn't looking at Aron. In fact, Aron was pretty sure Micah had never pulled his eyes from Charlie's face.

"Back the fuck off," Aron said, his panther's growl lacing every syllable.

"Shit," Reed muttered. "Lola, take Grace inside."

"Take Rieka in," Gray said, assumably to Nova.

"You guys are jerks," Nova said from somewhere to Aron's left.

Rustling preceded footsteps on the dry ground and gravel.

"Please," Charlie said, her hand tightening on Aron's arm.

The last thing Aron wanted to do was scare Charlie. But Micah was riling up his panther and Aron was struggling to hold onto his skin.

"Micah, please calm down," Callie said, touching her mate the way Charlie was touching Aron.

Normally, a mate's touch was enough to calm any Shifter. But something was different about Micah. He always looked like his wolf was right there on the edge, always fighting for dominance, always waiting to attack anyone he perceived a threat.

"If they end up fighting, is Cujo going to make an appearance?" Emory asked.

Aron had no idea who the hell Cujo was, but he better not get in the fucking way. This shit was going to happen, no matter how badly Aron didn't want it. Micah was trembling with the fight over his own skin.

People began to stand. Males asked their mates to back up. Gray tried to demand the two males go elsewhere or calm the fuck down. Colton was cussing them both for coming close to fighting with his pregnant female so close.

And then a breeze pushed through the area, ruffling Aron's hair. His clothes began to flap against him, and Micah's eyes widened.

A second later, Micah was lifted off his feet and tossed about ten feet behind the circle of chairs where he landed on his ass … hard.

"Micah!" Callie cried out as she rushed to his side.

"Holy shit," someone muttered. "She's like Hollyn."

Turning his entire body to look down at his sweet little Fairy, he couldn't help but to smile at the determined look on her face as she stood slowly, her eyes glued on Micah's face.

"They asked you not to fight with the babies here. And that female is *really* pregnant," Charlie said, jabbing a finger toward where Shawnee was hobbling away from the circle. "The only thing I was hiding is the fact I'm a Fairy. Because it's dangerous for others to know about me. So, thank you for making me have to reveal myself."

Ohhh. His mate was pissed.

"I didn't make you do shit," Micah said as he stood and brushed the dried leaves and grass from his pants. "All I did was ask you a question."

"You were going to fight my mate," Charlie said, her hands balled in fists.

Everyone was silent for about a heartbeat. Then a chorus of squeals erupted from every single female there. Nova and Lola came running over with the toddlers on their hips. Even the sweet, quiet Callie left her own mate to hug Charlie and congratulate her. They all barely bared Aron a glance and a smile.

"Why are you hugging me and not him?" Charlie asked. "He's in this, too."

"Oh please. He won't hug us. He won't even look at us."

Charlie looked back at Aron with a raised brow. Shit. Did she actually want him to go against everything he stood for and touch a mated female? And what the hell would the males do if he actually did that?

"It's not disrespectful to me," Charlie said with what sure as hell looked like a shit eating grin.

All the women turned to look at him. Peyton, the newest turned wolf, barked out a laugh. "You think hugging us is disrespectful?"

Aron looked to the males for help. They all shrugged and shook their heads. Where the hell were the rest of the panthers?

As if he conjured them with his thoughts, two vehicles pulled in, grabbing everyone's attention and taking it off him. Thank God.

The group as a whole ambled toward the vehicles as the door to Brax's Camaro opened and a large, black dog lunged from the back seat.

Charlie tensed as Polo, Campbell's Rottweiler, came bounding toward them.

"Uh," she said, grabbing his arm. She was scared of dogs? Really? She'd just put herself between two large Shifter males and blew one across the gathering with her wind.

"He's friendly," Aron reassured her.

Polo sensed her fear and slowed his approach, sitting at her feet and waiting for her to acknowledge him and give him a head rub.

"Since when do dogs like Shifters?" Charlie asked, tentatively reaching down and scratching behind Polo's ear.

"Polo's a little different," Campbell said as she wandered over. She looked around at everyone's faces. "I thought it was okay if I brought him."

"It is. You know the girls love him," Nova said.

Campbell looked around again. "Then why does everyone look so...intense?"

Emory and Reed exchanged a look. Reed snorted. "Because Micah decided to go all protective asshole again. And, apparently, Charlie's a Fairy and blew his ass about a hundred yards away with a big gust of wind."

"It wasn't a hundred yards. It was like ten feet," Charlie said, a beautiful pink touching her cheeks.

"You're a Fairy?" Shawnee asked. She looked up at her mate. "Did you know that?"

Colton shrugged. "Nope. I'd heard Hollyn found a family member, but that was it."

Shawnee rolled her eyes at her bear Shifter mate. "You didn't put two and two together?"

Colton helped his hugely pregnant mate lower into her chair. "I had other things on my mind." He pressed a kiss to the top of her head then lowered into the seat beside her.

The rest of the Pride settled into lawn chairs they brought while Polo the dog made a beeline for the little girls to play.

Even with the immediate stress of a fight with Micah over, Aron couldn't make himself relax. He trusted everyone there completely. But he hated the fact that everyone knew not only what Charlie was, but that she'd had to out herself.

But why? Why had she felt the need to stand against Micah? She barely knew the people there. Yet she basically opened herself up to protect the women and babies.

Or was she protecting Aron?

That thought both amused him and scared him. She wanted to start hunting with the panthers. Did that mean any time there was a threat against one of them she'd put herself in danger to protect them? He hadn't feared Micah would retaliate; the male would never hurt a female.

But a Rogue would have no qualms about it.

How the hell could he get her to stay home and be safe while they risked their lives to save women exactly like her?

And how the hell could he convince her it was her idea so he didn't have to be the asshole?

Even thinking that made him feel like a dick. He was trying to think of a way to gaslight her.

Fuck. He knew he'd be a shitty mate someday.

Chapter Five

Charlie kept looking over at Aron. He hadn't said a word to her since they'd left Big River territory. Was he mad because she'd revealed she was a Fairy? Wasn't it her choice whether she told anyone or not?

"Aron," she started, but snapped her mouth shut when he turned to look at her. His eyes were bright green. She felt as if his panther was looking at her instead of the man she was falling hard for. "Never mind."

He turned his attention back to the dark road ahead of them and remained silent the rest of the trip. When he pulled into Charlie's driveway, she half expected him to kick her out of the truck and peel out.

Instead, he stepped out from the driver's seat, took jerky steps around the hood, and let her out of her side, holding his hand out to help her down. He placed a gentle hand on the small of her back and guided her up her stairs and to her door.

But when she unlocked the front door, he stopped her from entering, raised his head to scent the air, then stepped back.

"What are you doing?"

"I know you feel safer when I'm here, but I'm staying out here tonight," he said, his bright eyes both unnerving her and enthralling her.

"Why? Are you mad at me? I didn't want that Micah guy to hurt you or the rest of your friends. You obviously love them."

His head wagged side to side. "It's not just that."

"But that's part of it."

A low growl trickled up his throat and he took a step back, shoving his hands deep in his pocket.

Charlie moved toward him. "Aron, what's going on? If we're going to do this mate thing, we have to be open with each other. Why are you mad at me?"

"I'm not mad at you," he said, that growl still present in his voice.

"Then tell me what's going on."

Propping her hands on her hips, she prepared herself for an argument, whether it was to defend her actions or plead her case.

"My panther wants to mark you. I don't think it's smart for me to stay inside tonight."

The air left Charlie's lungs in a rush of air. "What? You know you can't mark me."

"And that's why I need to stay out of your house and away from you for the night."

"Why does your panther want to mark me all of a sudden? We agreed we were mates last night and that didn't happen. What changed? Is this..." She waved her hand back and forth between them. "Mate bond thing safe for me?"

His nostrils flared as he inhaled deep and his eyes closed slowly.

"My panther is scared for you. And so am I."

Charlie's brows pinched together as she studied him. "Why? Because I revealed my magic?"

He nodded his head without opening his eyes.

"You said I could trust those people. You said I could trust you."

His eyes snapped open. They'd lost a little of their glow. "You can. I promise." He stepped closer and raised a hand as if to touch her but dropped it to his side.

"Then what's going on? Why does your panther want to mark me? Why are you scared to touch me? Why are you worried your friends know I'm Fae?"

"It's not so much that everyone knows. It's seeing your strength and skill firsthand that has me freaked out."

"Okay. First of all, that's not the first time you've seen my wind. Second, why would that freak you out at all? I know you're not scared of me."

"I'm scared of you getting hurt," he said as if it should be obvious.

How the hell would she get hurt? He wasn't making any sense. Unless...

"Wait a minute. Are you having second thoughts about us and you're trying to find a way out of it? Because if that's it, just go. I don't want you to feel like you have to be with me. I thought you–"

"That's not it. I don't know how you can think that would be it." His brows were low as he shook his head. "I told you you're everything to me. Why would you think I was looking for a way out?"

"Then tell me what's going on. You're not making any sense."

"You said you want to go hunting. Then you proved how strong your magic is tonight. And I will never tell you what you can and can't do. I'm terrified of you encountering the rogues again, but I hate being away from you and worry the whole time. Either way, I'm fucked."

Well damn. The last thing she wanted to do was make his life harder. She wanted to help him take out the traffickers, but she didn't want him distracted by her presence.

But he'd said he worried when he *wasn't* with her. She'd been so terrified of her own shadow for so long.

No wonder he worried when he wasn't watching over her. She'd shown him nothing but her weakness for the last six weeks.

She'd forgotten she had her magic to protect herself. She'd vowed to never be caught off guard again.

"I'm not scared anymore, Aron." Lie. Partial lie, anyway. She was still scared but refused to let the memory of what happened to her control her life.

"Charlie—"

"Nope. You're going to come inside. We're going to hang out and watch some TV. Then we're going to bed."

"I can't sleep in bed with you."

"Fine. I'll make you a bed on the floor. But you're not sleeping like you did last night. That looked super uncomfortable."

A smile finally cracked his lips. She could've sighed with relief. For a second there, she wondered if she truly knew Aron or if she'd built up this perfect person in her head. Okay, yeah. She knew he wasn't perfect.

But he was perfect for her.

Aron helped her pull extra blankets and an old bedspread along with a few pillows out of the hall closet. Together, they built him a softer, warmer bed beside hers. He protested, saying it was still too close, but Charlie refused to budge on this.

"If you won't sleep up here beside me," she said as she sat on the edge of the bed, "at least you can sleep nearby. And not outside my door like a dog."

He snorted as he tried to hold in a laugh. "Cat."

"What?"

"I'm a cat. Not a dog."

Charlie tried. She really did. But the laugh burst through her lips before she could stop it. Then the giggles started until tears rolled down her cheeks.

Aron chuckled along with her. "Why is that so funny?"

She inhaled a few times, trying to get the hysterics under control. Wiping her cheeks, she spoke through her laughter. "I was picturing you stretching and sleeping on the end of my bed."

He shook his head and chuckled again. "Don't worry. I won't pee on anything while you sleep."

Aaaand the hysterical laughter was back.

****

Aron wasn't sure how long they joked and laughed. But eventually, Charlie grew quiet. And then her breathing became slow and steady as sleep dragged her into dreams. He hoped they were good dreams and not the nightmares that had plagued her for the past couple months.

Laying on his side, he stared at the edge of the bed and listened to her soft breathing. He'd wanted to lie beside her. He'd wanted to hold her in his arms as she slept. But he didn't trust himself or his panther. One bite could kill her. And after seeing her magic in full display tonight, and knowing she wanted to hunt along with the rest of the Pride, his panther grew more and more possessive as the night grew on.

Fucking Micah. Everything had been fine until he'd shown his ass. Why couldn't they bring a new person into the fold without him getting all weird?

At least they'd had a good night when they'd gotten back to her house. She'd teased and played. Her laugh was like music to his fucking ears. He could've listened to her giggles for the rest of his life, even if they were at his expense.

He didn't mind. It wasn't like she was insulting him. She was simply slaphappy after weeks without good sleep. And then she'd held her own like a champ when surrounded by all his friends and his Pride.

She'd been amazing.

Why had her display upset his panther so much? Was it because both sides of Aron realized she truly wasn't some damsel in distress?

Was it because they saw her strength and couldn't find a good reason as to why she shouldn't join them on their quest to end the fucking Rogues?

He wasn't sure. And there was a good chance he'd never get an answer, either.

As he listened to Charlie sleeping, his eyes grew heavy. Even on his makeshift cot on the floor, he was so much more at ease being near her. He'd texted Daxon to let the rest of the panthers know he wouldn't be home again tonight. The asshole had razzed him, but whatever.

Had anyone told the panthers about the announcement of mating with Charlie? They hadn't been there. But, surely, they'd known all along. Hence their giving her distance whenever they were around her. Also why they made very little eye contact with her.

Maybe Charlie and Campbell were right. It was an antiquated way of thinking. How was simply touching, talking, or looking at a mated female considered disrespectful? All the females he knew thought the panthers were aloof, or that they didn't like them. That couldn't be further from the truth.

If he changed, it would take a lot of time and effort. And that was a big *if*. He wouldn't tell the panthers they had to change their ways, but it might be time for Aron to form closer bonds with the females he knew, loved, and respected.

Sleep claimed him as he made up his mind to make an effort to get closer to the women in the various Packs, Clans, and Prides.

And with sleep came fucking nightmares.

This one was his least favorite and had come to him so many nights after he'd met Charlie.

They were running through the woods, the sound of a battle up ahead. Campbell had split from the group and was flanking them from the other side. A feminine scream broke through the snarls and growls.

Aron pushed his panther to run faster. Even in the dream, Aron knew the female up ahead was important to him. In his nightmares, he could never remember her name, could never remember who she was, but always knew her face immediately.

Charlie's hands were up as she tried to call her wind forward. Unlike what had happened in reality, her magic never came. As he watched, as he ran as fast as his legs would take him, one of the wolf

Shifters clamped his teeth around her throat and shook her like a rag doll.

By the time his Pride got to her side, she was dead, her lifeless eyes staring up at the starry sky.

Aron always woke hard from that nightmare. Sweat drenched his t-shirt and boxers as his breathing came in ragged breaths.

"Nightmare?" Charlie's soft voice broke through the darkness of her room.

He grunted in response as he tried to remind himself she'd lived, that she was lying a few feet from him.

"Want to talk about it?"

"No," he croaked out.

Fabric swished and the mattress creaked.

And then Charlie was pulling his blanket up and sliding in beneath it, her warm body pressed against his from shoulder to thigh.

"Me neither."

He turned his head to look at her in the dark. He could see at night as clearly as he could on a cloudy day, except colors were muted to grays.

"You have a nightmare, too?" His voice was scratchy. "Did I talk in my sleep?"

"You roared. Or your panther did."

His brows shot to his hairline. That was what woke her up. "Sorry I woke you."

"I was already awake. I had a nightmare, too."

"About that night?" he asked, and gave in to temptation. Rolling onto his side, he draped an arm across her waist. The simple touch settled his panther until he purred.

"Yeah. Only you died."

Aron felt his eyes go wide. They'd dreamed almost the exact same thing, only the situation had been reversed.

And she'd called it a nightmare, too. Why was he surprised? She'd told him how she felt about him. Told him her magic had been pulling toward him since that first night.

"You're sweaty," she whispered as she dragged her fingers softly up and down his arm.

Charlie turned onto her side so his arm was over her waist. She laid an arm on his hip so it was like they were hugging while lying down.

With her so close and in his arms, sleep dragged him under again quickly. And this time, there were no nightmares.

No dreams.

Just rest.

****

When Charlie woke again, she found herself curled against Aron, her head resting on his shoulder, his arms wrapped tightly around her. She didn't want to get up.

But her bladder and her stomach said otherwise.

Extricating herself slowly and carefully from Aron's embrace, she tiptoed from the room and pulled the door closed behind her as quietly as possible. After using the bathroom, she headed for the kitchen, got the coffee going, and made a simple breakfast of cereal. If Aron was hungry, she'd make him something bigger. But she'd lived alone so long she rarely cooked for herself anymore, living on frozen meals, cereal, and take out.

It wasn't that she couldn't cook. She just didn't see the point of cooking and making a mess for only her.

But it wasn't only her now.

She had Aron. And Hollyn. And a huge group of new friends.

"Oh man," she muttered to herself.

Did everyone fear her now? After her display of magic, after throwing their friend across the field, would they all hate her? Would they be reluctant to have her around?

No way. When she'd wanted to leave, Emory and the rest of the group begged her to stay. And they'd all included her in the conversation, even after the incident with the surly Shifter.

She'd been disappointed that Hollyn hadn't made an appearance last night, but she'd texted saying the bar had gotten too busy. The pregnant female, Shawnee, used to be a waitress there before she got so big. And now it was only Noah and Hollyn working the entire place.

Charlie understood. She was sad she didn't get to see her cousin, but at least she now knew where to find her.

That actually sounded good today. She wanted to see if Aron would be up to going to Moe's to hang out with Hollyn and get lunch.

Oh wait. It was Monday. Did Aron have to work? She wasn't even sure where he worked. They'd declared their feelings for each other, yet they barely knew each other.

But did that matter? Nope. People fell in love for other reasons and it had nothing to do with career choices, finances, or even looks. She'd fallen in love with Aron because he was strong and noble. He was gentle and kind and so dang brave. She'd never met anyone who was so willing to risk his own life to save complete strangers.

Aron's world was amazing. The people in his life were amazing.

The more she thought about all of them, the more she found she wanted them in her life, too. She wanted to be a part of that big, silly crew. And she found herself unafraid of them, even though they were Shifters. Even though some of them were wolf Shifters, just like the ones who'd taken her and so many other women.

Amazing. All of them.

She wanted to be like them. She wanted to be a part of something bigger than herself. She wanted to leave her mark on the world rather than staying in hiding for as long as she stayed alive. And staying alive was quite a feat for someone of her kind.

Her cereal bowl propped in her hands, her coffee mug sitting on the coffee table, she curled her legs under her on the couch and glanced toward the closed door.

She'd woken up to a terrible nightmare, then heard a bone rattling roar come from the floor. It had startled her, but, oddly enough, it hadn't frightened her. She wasn't scared of Aron or his panther. The moment she'd heard the sound it felt like her magic knew exactly who and what it was. It was a cry of anguish.

And then she'd crawled under the blanket with him. He'd been a complete gentleman and simply held her all night despite his fear he'd bite her.

Charlie sighed. Her life had taken such a turn over the past few months. From absolute terror and chaos to complete and total happiness. She felt like she'd found where she was supposed to be, *who* she was supposed to be.

Finishing her cereal, she set the empty bowl on the table as her doorknob turned and Aron exited.

"I was going to wake you up soon. I wasn't sure if you had to work today or not," she said as his eyes met hers.

He shook his head with a grunt. "Coffee?"

"Yep. I'll get it. Sugar or cream? Milk?"

"Black," he said as he dropped heavily onto the couch beside her.

Charlie leaned over and pressed a quick kiss to his cheek then lunged from the couch and made him a cup of coffee, carrying it over with a smile.

"Oh god," he muttered as he brought the mug to his lips for a sip.

"What?" she asked, frowning at him as she resumed her position on the couch with her legs folded under her.

"You're a morning person."

Charlie smiled wide and nodded. "Always have been. Even when I'm tired, I tend to have a bunch of energy when I wake up."

Aron dropped his head back against the couch and held the mug in both hands. "Did you get any more sleep after I freaked out?"

"You didn't freak out. Your panther was simply talking in his sleep…your sleep. How does that work, anyway?"

He rolled his head on the cushion to look at her. "How does what work?"

"Does your panther know what you're thinking and vice versa? Or is it just you in panther form?"

"Both. Yes."

"Huh?"

"We know what each other is thinking. I'm my panther, but my panther is also me. We have a dual side. He thinks autonomously but I'm in control."

"I'm not sure that cleared it up. But I'll give you a break since you're obviously grumpy in the morning."

Aron rolled his eyes, shook his head, and dropped it back against the cushion. "Did you eat?" he asked.

"Yep. Had some cereal. You hungry?"

"What time is it?" he asked without opening his eyes.

"Uhhh." She picked up her phone and checked. "Eleven thirty-six."

She'd slept late two days in a row. She felt great. Maybe she'd put some more meat on her bones now, too. She'd always been on the thin side, but she knew she'd lost entirely too much weight over the past six weeks.

"Moe's is open. Noah and your cousin should be there. I want a burger."

He stood without another word, set his mug on the coffee table, and shuffled into her bathroom. Seconds later, the squeak of her faucet let her know he was taking a shower. Did he bring any clean clothes, or would he put the same ones on again?

He'd done that yesterday then gone home to change before they headed to Big River territory. If he was going to stay with Charlie more often, he needed to keep a few changes of clothes and a toothbrush here so he didn't have to wear dirty clothes.

While he was showering, Charlie headed into her room to get dressed. She pulled a clean pair of jeans and a sweatshirt from her closet and pulled off her pajamas. As she was tossing them in the hamper, a gasp brought her attention to her bedroom door.

Aron stood there in nothing but a towel, his wide eyes roaming her from head to toe. She barely had a second to cover her bare breasts before his gaze zeroed in on them.

"Shit. I'm sorry." He promptly gave her his back.

Pulling on a bra as fast as she could, she tugged her sweatshirt over her head then yanked the jeans up her legs and over her hips.

"Okay. I'm dressed," she said, her cheeks blazing with heat.

But she realized the heat wasn't only from embarrassment. Aron looked downright edible. Water beads stood on his chest and back where he hadn't dried off enough. His wet hair looked darker and was messy. The towel accented the V of his hips and highlighted the dusting of dark hair that trailed to what she could only imagine was a promise of ecstasy.

"I'll give you some privacy," she said, hurrying past him and pulling the door closed behind her.

As she leaned against the closed door, she remembered his words from two days ago. Anything that happened would be on her timeline. She'd have to make the first move for anything and everything they did, even their first kiss.

Did she have the guts to walk in her room, pull that towel from his waist, and take control of his body?

As her own body warmed and her blood heated, she realized not only did she have the guts but a need so deep it made her dizzy. When was the last time she'd made love with a man? When was the last time she'd been touched? When was the last time she'd felt a world-shattering orgasm?

That last question was easy to answer – she'd never felt an earth-shattering orgasm. She'd had fun and felt the beginnings of a release, but she'd never been with a man who made sure she finished before he did.

Would Aron be like that? She couldn't picture Aron as a selfish lover. She pictured him as selfless and passionate and –

"Sorry about that," he said as he pulled the door open.

Charlie flew backward and landed in Aron's arms as he caught her before she hit the floor.

"Oh man," she groaned, raising one hand to cover her face. And now she was on fire for a whole other reason.

"You okay?" he asked, setting her upright. "What were you doing? Did you think I was going to go through your drawers or something?"

There was a teasing glint in his eyes. But she also felt as if he knew exactly why she'd been outside the door, leaning against it like a weirdo.

"I'm fine," she said, straightening the hem of her sweatshirt and doing everything she could to avoid eye contact. "You ready to go?"

"Hey," he said, tucking a finger under her chin and lifting so she had to look at him. "What's wrong? Are you upset because I saw you naked?"

"I wasn't naked. I was only a little naked."

"You were pretty naked." That crooked grin she'd grown to love was present on the lips she so badly wanted to taste again.

"I'm not mad you saw me naked."

"Then what's up?" he said, releasing his hold and taking a step out of her space.

"I wanted to come in there with you."

His brows puckered and he looked behind him at her messy bedroom.

"You wanted to come in the bedroom with me?"

"I wanted to come in there and yank that towel from your hips."

The second the last word left her lips, Aron's arms snaked around her back and pulled her close.

"Is this okay?" he asked, his voice deep and hoarse.

"It's more than okay," she said, wrapping a hand around his neck and pulling his head down so she could press her lips to his.

The kiss quickly turned hungry.

They'd kissed twice already. But this one...this one boiled her blood and curled her toes.

Threading her fingers through his hair, she pulled him closer, pressed her body closer until her breasts were firmly against his hard chest. His erection pressed against her belly and Charlie had the urge to jump up and wrap her legs around his waist.

So...she did.

Aron's arms reached out and hooked under her ass as though he knew exactly what she was thinking. Maybe he did. Maybe he had the exact same desires she did.

And that was for him to carry her back to her unmade bed, lay her on the mattress, and strip her clothes from her body.

But then Aron pulled back, pulling a frustrated moan from Charlie.

"Are you sure? I don't want you to think –"

She silenced his concerns with her lips, swallowing any protest he might have had.

He was worried she would regret it. She knew that. But she wanted nothing more than to feel his hands on her body, his weight above her, pushing her down onto the bed.

One of Aron's hands left her ass and cupped the back of her head, his fingers tunneling through her hair. She could kiss him all day. As much as she wanted to feel him inside her, just the feeling of his body against hers and his tongue warring with hers made her dizzy.

No. She needed more. She definitely needed all of him.

Air breezed past her as Aron turned them and headed back into her bedroom. He kicked the door shut behind him even though they were the only ones there. For some reason, that little move drove her need even more.

He turned and sat with Charlie straddling him, one hand in her hair, the other still cradling her butt. She would have to make every first move.

So be it.

Pulling her hands from his hair and neck, she reached between them and grabbed the bottom hem of his shirt, pulling up until he had to break the kiss so she could remove it.

And then she sat there staring at him.

He was perfection. A freaking Adonis. His muscles were defined and chiseled without being too bulky. He was strength and sinew and flawless.

And she was still a little on the thin side with smaller boobs. What would he think when she was naked?

Insecurities dampened her mood a tad.

Until he reached down and yanked her shirt over her head, tossing it across the room.

His eyes immediately flashed bright green as he stared down at her bra clad breasts.

"Damn," he breathed, dipping his head to kiss her collarbone, between her breasts, then the swell of each. "What the hell did I do to deserve you?" His tone was so reverent and sweet all thoughts of his rejection of her body fled her brain immediately.

Aron stood and turned again, laying her gently on the mattress, and then stood there staring down at her. She had the urge to cover up, but if they were going to commit to each other the way they'd said he'd see a lot more of her a lot more often.

His hands trembled as they reached down and popped the button on his jeans. The rip of his zipper lowering was drowned out by the sharp breaths sawing in and out of her lungs.

When he pushed his jeans down his hips, her mouth instantly watered. He wore no underwear, no boxers, nothing to obscure her view from his rather impressive erection that jutted toward her and gleamed at the tip.

"Wow," she breathed out.

Her eyes raised back to his face to find a boyish grin raising one side of his lips. Was that insecurity in his own eyes? What the hell did he have to be insecure about?

Reaching down to her own pants, she hesitated when Aron raised a hand. "Let me," he said.

Kneeling on the bed, he unfastened her pants and slowly peeled them down her legs, hooking his fingers in her panties and pulling then off at the same time. And then he ogled her the way she'd ogled him. Shaking his head, he sighed and lowered to plant small kisses along her shins and thighs.

And she was thankful she'd taken the time to shave.

Pushing her legs apart, his tongue took a long swipe through her folds, making her eyes roll into the back of her head. He spent more time there, teasing, licking, sucking, making love to her core with his mouth until she was writhing on the bed and clenching the sheets in her hands.

It only took minutes of his oral ministrations for her to fall over the edge with a long, loud moan.

Aron kissed and sucked until the last of the aftershocks faded, then raised up her body.

When he sat back, he looked over his shoulder.

"What?" she asked.

"My wallet is in my jeans."

She frowned up at him in confusion.

"Condom," he said with a smirk and a shrug.

Charlie watched him rip the foil package open with his teeth. He gripped his shaft in one hand while using the other to roll the rubber down his length. It was by far one of the sexiest things she'd ever seen.

Aron lowered himself back down, positioning the head of his cock against her opening.

"Are you sure?" he asked again, holding himself up on his arms, the tendons and muscles flexing.

She raised her hips, taking him in slowly in answer.

A deep moan trickled from Aron's lips and the beautiful green iridescence in his eyes grew brighter, something she didn't know was possible.

He was so slow, so gentle as he rolled his hips and pushed forward until he was fully sheathed inside of her. Her body stretched to accommodate the intrusion. It had been so long since she'd been intimate with a man that it took more than a few seconds.

Aron dropped down onto his elbows and kissed her sweetly, his lips lingering as he pulled from her then pushed back in slowly.

"I love you," he whispered as he looked into her eyes.

"I love you, too."

His hips kept making those agonizingly slow movements until she almost begged him to take her harder, faster, to make her scream out with release.

She didn't need to say a word.

Burying his head in the crook of her neck, he left tiny kisses on her shoulder as his tempo increased, shaking the mattress, making the old springs beneath her squeak.

After a few minutes, Aron shifted his weight until he was on his knees with her legs over the crooks of his elbows. From this position, his cock went so much deeper and Charlie could feel the first tingles of another release forming.

"Aron," she moaned as his pace became more frenzied, needier, hungrier.

He hooked both legs over one arm and bent forward, cupping one of her breasts in his free hand, kneading it, then pinched her pebbled nipple between his finger and thumb.

That pushed her over the edge.

Opening her mouth, she cried out as an orgasm crashed through her, sending stars shooting off behind her closed lids.

Aron thrust into her harder, faster, until he called out her name and followed her over the cliff.

He slowed, each pump of his hips pulling aftershocks from her and causing her to twitch until she became sensitive.

Lowering her legs to the bed, Aron stretched out on top of her, keeping himself fully sheathed inside of her. He held his weight on his elbows again and pressed kisses to her forehead, her cheeks, even the tip of her nose before pressing his lips to hers.

"I love you so much."

Charlie raised her hand and cupped his stubbled cheek. "I love you, Aron."

Never in her life had she felt so sated, so content, and so loved.

Chapter Six

Aron smiled and shook his head as Charlie dove into her burger like she hadn't eaten in weeks. In reality, she hadn't. He couldn't wait to see her at a healthy weight. She was the most beautiful woman he'd ever seen no matter what she weighed, but he knew she was malnourished and tired.

Especially after the hour they'd spent exploring each other's bodies. They'd had sex two more times before succumbing to their hunger and having to take a time out for food.

She'd been amazing and passionate and so damn sexy. He'd let her make the first move, but only barely. When she had told him she'd wanted to rip the towel from his waist, he'd pulled her to his body. And then let her set the pace.

It had taken every ounce of restraint to keep from sinking his teeth in her shoulder when they'd made love the last time. His panther had pushed a partial Shift and his mouth had filled with fangs. Which was why he'd rolled them over and let her take the lead. It was way harder for him to reach her when she was straddling his hips.

"Aren't you hungry?" she asked when she caught him watching her.

"Just thinking," he said. Wasn't a lie. He was thinking and fantasizing and wondering when the next time he would feel her body beneath his hands again.

"You keep staring at me. Do I have something on my face?" She grabbed a napkin and wiped.

"Nope. You're beautiful. You blame me for staring?" He picked up his burger and took a big bite, smiling around the food when her cheeks flushed bright pink.

Hollyn stepped through the front door, her eyes squinted from going from the bright sun to the dim light of the bar.

"Hey!" she said, her voice and face full of excitement when she spotted Charlie. "Sorry I couldn't make it yesterday. We were slammed."

Charlie stood and stepped into Hollyn's outstretched arms. They hugged for minutes, pulling away but keeping a hand on each other like they'd done the first night they'd seen each other again.

"I got to get the bar set up, but you're going to stick around for a while, right?"

Charlie looked to Aron with raised brows.

"Yeah. We'll stay for a while," he said, lifting his iced tea in a salute.

"Want some help?" Charlie asked, a wide grin on her face.

"Nah. I've got it. Finish your lunch. I'll come back over when I'm finished if it doesn't pick up."

Noah waited for his mate, lifting the flap on the side for her to enter. "You're late," he teased, slapping her ass as she passed.

Charlie turned back to Aron, that wide grin still in place. "You really don't mind if we stay for a bit?"

"Not at all." Especially not when it made her so happy. He would turn the world upside down if it meant he'd see that smile all day.

They ended up staying longer than a bit. Hours passed, people came and went, and then it was time for dinner.

"We can leave if you want," Charlie said around a mouthful of fries.

Aron chuckled as he shook his head. "We can stay as late as you want."

Anytime the bar slowed down, or everyone had their drinks, Hollyn made a point to head straight to their table. Aron loved watching the two women talk, laugh, and catch up on everything they had done for the past ten years.

The other members of Ravenwood Pride stepped through the door, their eyes scanning the room before settling on where Aron, Charlie, and Hollyn sat.

"Hey," Daxon said as he lowered beside Aron. "When did you two get here?"

Charlie glanced over at Daxon with a smile. "Around twelve." Then she turned back to her conversation with her cousin.

Daxon raised his brows high. "Y'all have been here all day?"

Aron shrugged and nodded toward Charlie. He didn't need to say anything else. Even if Brax was the only other male in the Pride who was mated, every single panther would do anything to make a female happy.

Especially if that female happened to be his mate.

The males nodded. Campbell smiled and rolled her eyes. "You boys can act as tough as you want, but you're all a bunch of softies." She lowered into the chair beside Charlie and bumped her with her shoulder. "Hey girl."

Charlie bumped her back and smiled. "How are you?"

"Good. Starving. Someone," Campbell said, narrowing her eyes playfully at her mate, Brax, "kept me so busy all day I didn't get to eat."

"I don't remember hearing you complain," Brax teased back.

Pink flushed bright on Campbell's cheeks. Ducking her head, she hid her smile. By that smile, he assumed their earlier activities weren't suitable for public conversation. Good thing Nova wasn't here. She would've tried her damnedest to get details.

"What do you guys want to eat?" Hollyn asked, rising to stand.

"I'll get it," Noah said as he neared the table. He bent and pressed a kiss to the top of Hollyn's head. "What do you assholes and Campbell want?"

Campbell grinned wide up at Noah. "Thanks," she said.

Noah took everyone's orders, giving his mate time to hang out with her long-lost cousin longer. The smile Charlie shot Noah was full of gratitude and so damn beautiful.

"What are you two up to today?" Campbell asked once Noah left the table.

"You're looking at it," Aron said, nodding at Noah for another beer. He probably should've mentioned that when he was at the table. Noah apparently thought so, too.

"Come up and get it. I was just over there," Noah grumbled in his typical gruff tone.

"I'll get it," Charlie said, pushing to her feet.

"Sit. Hang out with Hollyn. I'll get it."

He gently pushed her back into her chair with both hands on her shoulders.

Charlie smiled up at him as he passed. "Could you get me a beer?"

She'd been drinking sweet tea since they'd arrived over four hours ago. And she hadn't had a beer the first night she'd come to Moe's, or when they'd hung out with the wolves and beers. She was finally letting loose.

Hopefully, that meant she was growing to trust the Shifters more. Or at least he hoped she was trusting him and his friends more. Hell. Even *he* didn't trust all Shifters.

Aron grabbed a bucket of beers. And then another. Two hours later, the table had finished four buckets and several rounds of shots.

While it took more alcohol than normal for Shifters to get drunk because of their high temperature and metabolism, that obviously wasn't the case for Charlie and Campbell. Both women were highly buzzed and had a case of the giggles.

This was a whole new side of Charlie. Every second he got to know her more, he fell even harder for the beautiful Fairy, who caught him staring and winked at him.

He wanted her so bad. He wanted to spend another hour touching her, kissing her, licking her, and making her moan. The mere memory of this morning made him hard.

"Dude," Mason said from beside Daxon. "I'm gonna guess by the way you're staring at her and how bright your eyes are glowing you two finally–"

"Don't say it," Aron warned. He might not be a typical Alpha, but he was still Alpha. And he'd kick anyone's ass for disrespecting his mate.

Mason was different from the rest of the panthers. He teased and joked with Campbell and Charlie. Even some of the mates of his friends. While it might not be to the same degree as other males, he still interacted with the opposite sex far more than the rest of them.

The door opened and in poured a few more bodies. Two of the bears from Blackwater and their mates, along with a couple of the wolves and their mates. No Gray and Nova. No Reed and Lola. No Colton and Shawnee.

As he watched the Shifters without kids, he wondered if the others were jealous of their freedom. Would he rather have the life he had now, or fill it with cubs?

The answer was easy – fill it with cubs. But only if Charlie was their mother.

Would they be cubs? Or Fae? He had no idea how that worked. Noah and Hollyn hadn't begun a family yet, and he sure as hell wasn't going to reach out to the Shifter Council for answers. He'd never fully trusted them.

Guess they'd have to wait and find out.

That is if she wanted a family. They'd only been committed to each other, if that's what it could be called, for a couple of days. It was a little early for that conversation.

"Hey!" Emory said as she walked over, bent at the waist, and hugged Charlie. "Good to see you again."

"Do you all come here every night?" Charlie asked, watching as each person crossed to her to hug her or nodded their hello.

"Pretty much," Peyton said as she sat in the chair Tristan pulled out for her.

Peyton's mate, Tristan, rarely spoke. Aron had his assumptions as to why, but it was his business. If Tristan didn't want to talk, that was his prerogative. Aron hadn't been much of a talker before Campbell had come along and tried to force everyone into conversations. Then Charlie really loosened his tongue.

In more ways than one.

The newcomers ordered a few buckets of beer and settled in, treating Charlie as if she'd been a part of this group for years rather than days. Fuck, he had some awesome friends.

Another hour passed and Charlie requested a shot.

"You sure about that?" Aron asked, leaning over to whisper in her ear. "You're a little drunk already."

"Yeah. But have you seen what my cousin can do?"

Of course he had. That was one of the reasons Moe's had become even more popular and why humans, like Peyton was before she'd been Turned, ended up in this place.

With a nod, he ordered a shot for him and Charlie. Noah waved him off when he tried to hand him his debit card. "On the house," he grumbled.

"What kind does she want?" Hollyn asked, looking to her cousin and shaking her head when Charlie gave her a wide grin and two thumbs up.

"I think she just wants to see you perform."

"Alrighty then," Hollyn said, then grabbed bottles and got to work.

As she flipped and twirled bottles and blew flames with the liquor – only a handful of them knew that was her magic and not a bartending trick – the bar went nuts, chanting, whistling, even howling.

Aron turned to watch his mate; she had the most beautiful smile and a twinkle in her eye as she watched intently. Aron was so distracted by her expression he'd almost missed the door opening and closing behind him. Glancing in the mirror, he realized the newcomers were familiar.

And not welcome.

Turning to face the members of Black Feather Crew, he refrained from immediately checking on Charlie. Black Feather thrived on that kind of shit. The second they realized someone they didn't like had a mate or even a female of interest, they did everything in their power to stir up trouble.

He hated those fuckers.

As if on cue, the room was permeated with the scent of fur. Which meant the entire table of his people had noticed Black Feather's arrival.

"Shit," Noah muttered from behind the bar. "What the fuck are you doing here?" His tone was full of warning.

"Same as everyone else. Here for the beer and the show," Jacob, the Alpha of Black Feather Crew, said.

A low growl trickled from the back of the room. Jacob glanced toward Aron's table and smirked. When he looked back, he caught Aron staring.

"What the fuck you looking at?"

"Tough guy," Aron said under his breath as he snatched the shots from the bar top and carried it over to where everyone sat.

"I like how you insulted me under your breath and ran away like a coward," Jacob said.

"He's a pussy cat. What did you expect?" Clint, the Second of the Crew, said.

Aron could feel his panther straining to break free. But there wasn't a chance in hell he'd fight these assholes. Not in Noah's bar. Not in front of his mate. Not in front of so many females.

He had more respect than that.

Control was quickly becoming an issue, though. Especially when Jacob's eyes zeroed in on Charlie when she leaned against Aron and snatched her shot from the tray.

The look Jacob gave Aron told him exactly how the night was going to go. And it wasn't fucking good.

****

Charlie had had way too much to drink. She was fully aware of that. But she couldn't remember the last time she'd had so much fun. She was pretty sure Hollyn spent more time at her table than behind the bar. But the big guy behind the bar – Hollyn's mate, as her cousin had so proudly announced – didn't seem to mind one bit.

Aron's friends treated Charlie as if she'd been with them for years. They included her in the conversations, all the inside jokes, even teased her a bit. She loved it. She loved this big crazy group. And already, she considered them all family and was growing mildly protective of them. Even if the guys were huge and the women all seemed like total badasses.

Hollyn had agreed to show off her skills behind the bar and prepared a round of shots after flipping the bottles around and blowing fire. What would the place think if they knew she hadn't used alcohol but her own magic?

Shame Charlie couldn't use her magic to make a living. Wasn't like anyone hired people who could create storms or tornadoes.

The thought made her snort with a barely held back chuckle.

"What?" Emory asked, leaning over to hear the joke.

"Nothing. Just thinking," Charlie said, her eyes on Aron's ass as he made his way to the front to retrieve the drinks.

Her man sure was sexy. After the time they'd had this afternoon, she was dying for another round with the hunk of man who was now glaring at some guys who'd walked through the door.

Wait. Why was he glaring?

Charlie couldn't hear what they were saying over the loud conversation and the music coming from the jukebox. But whatever was going on wasn't friendly.

The guy Aron had been talking to looked her way but didn't seem to notice her. It looked as if he were inventorying the table. There were four other guys with him, but who cared? At her table were big bear Shifters, a lion Shifter, wolf Shifters, and according to Aron's friends, the female Peyton had a crazy wolf inside of her.

Oh. And there were two Fae in the building who could blow their asses out into the parking lot then roast them where they stood.

The thought of someone upsetting her mate had her feeling all kinds of violent.

As Aron rejoined her, a tray filled with shot glasses in one of his hands, Charlie smiled wide at him.

"Want me to blow them outside?"

Aron's brows crashed down. "I'm pretty sure I know what you meant, but maybe rephrase that before my panther bursts free and tears them to shreds."

Charlie frowned up at him in confusion.

Emory burst out laughing beside her. "You totally just said you would blow them outside."

"Yeah?"

Emory crudely made a blow job motion with her mouth and hand.

"Oh! That's totally not what I meant." Her cheeks were hot as everyone gawked at her or laughed outright at her faux pas. "I just meant I'd—"

"Not everyone here knows everything," Aron said, leaning so close his lips brushed her ear and sent a shiver down her spine.

"If I keep saying stupid stuff, will you do that again?"

Aron pulled back and shook his head. "You've had a lot to drink," he said, pushing her shot toward her. "You can hold off on that for a while if you want."

"I won't puke," she said, lifting her shot in the air and waiting for everyone else to join her.

"I like her," Emory said. Lifting her shot, she *tinked* it against Charlie's. "To our new friend," she declared.

The entire table lifted their shots and repeated the toast. Heat rushed her cheeks again, but this time she didn't bother ducking her gaze. She wasn't used to this much attention, but it was out of love. These people would never hurt her, nor would they let anyone else.

But those jackasses who had come in were glaring at the males at the table. They leered at the women, too, but only when they knew the mates were watching.

Shit disturbers. That's what they were. Their mere presence irritated her. She half expected her magic to surge forward, but it never came. It appeared she had had too much to drink.

While she'd offered to use her magic to make those jerks leave, she now wasn't sure she would even be able to access it if she needed it. The thought made her uneasy. She didn't like the feeling of being so vulnerable again. It brought all those old feelings rushing back again.

"Should we go?" Charlie whispered into Aron's ear.

"Do you want to go?" His dark blonde brows were low.

"Are they...dangerous?" she asked, nodding her head the slightest bit toward the group of men still staring in their direction.

"They're a bunch of assholes. But I would never let anything happen to you."

"I know that. But I don't want a fight in your friend's bar."

Aron rested a hand on Charlie's leg under the table and squeezed enough to lend her some of his strength. "Noah hates them, too."

"Then why did he let them in?"

Aron rolled his eyes and shrugged up one shoulder. "Bad business to refuse anyone you dislike. Unless they do something to cause a problem, he'll let them stay here and drink. If they cause an issue, he'll kick them out. Won't be the first jackoffs he's barred."

He lifted the beer to his lips, but she didn't miss his eyes darting to the group of men making comments now.

"Talk big when you're across the room," Micah said. His eyes were bright, and he looked even more intense than usual.

"Don't start shit," Emory said.

Charlie looked around the table; she wasn't the only one who'd noticed the way the newcomers leered at the women. All the males' eyes were bright as though their animals fought for dominance.

"Did you want us to join you?" a guy asked.

Micah's eyes flashed even brighter, if that was at all possible. Aron's hand began to tremble on her thigh as his grip tightened. She reached down and pried his fingers away before he left a bruise on her pale skin.

"Aron," she whispered.

From the corner of her eye, she saw one guy lean toward another and say something into his ear. Her magic might not have been cooperating, but it was definitely warning her something wasn't right about those guys.

"Who are they? Why don't you like them?" Charlie whispered as softly as she could, keeping her mouth near his ear in hopes the other Shifters wouldn't hear her talking.

Aron's nostrils flared as he turned to look into her eyes. "Black Feather Crew. Crow Shifters. And total assholes," he said, not bothering to keep his voice low.

The men cackled and lifted their beers in a weird salute. "That your girl?" one guy asked Aron.

Turning in his seat, he glared at the one who'd spoken. "Get the fuck out of here, Clint."

Clint. Even his name sounded like a jerk. Okay. That wasn't fair. Surely, not all Clints were assholes. But this guy sure was. He was goading Aron. As were the rest of his friends. It was like they were trying to get everyone riled up so they'd fight.

"Nah. I think I'll stick around. Too many hot chicks to leave just yet." Clint leaned back in his seat and took a long pull of his beer, then smiled wide at Aron.

Originally, Charlie had wanted to leave. She wanted to avoid the drama. Now? Now all those emotions that had been dragged back by their arrival came rearing back and ticked her off.

"Why don't you shut up and mind your business," she said. Or slurred. Yeah. Her words were definitely slurred with the large amount of alcohol she'd drank.

"Ohhh!" another guy said as the others laughed. "Careful. The little human is getting mad."

Human? They thought she was human? That was probably for the best. They seemed like the kind of Shifters she'd spent her entire life avoiding.

And being as her magic was apparently as drunk as Charlie was, there wasn't a whole lot she could do to help if the room erupted in fur and teeth.

"Shut the fuck up or get out!" Noah boomed from the bar. A couple Shifters winced with the noise, but Charlie caught herself smirking at the crow Shifters.

It appeared the alcohol was lending her a little courage. She was still worried about a fight breaking out, but for some reason, she couldn't find any fear toward a group of men who turned into birds.

Ha! It would be cats against birds. No way would those guys win.

A couple of the crows lifted their hands with smiles as if they were surrendering but didn't really mean it. Jerks. No. Assholes. That was what Aron had called them and that was what they were.

Even drunk, she could tell they were nothing but trouble. They were probably like the rogues and believed women were beneath them.

Yep. Total and complete assholes.

Chapter Seven

The crows didn't say much else to Aron or Charlie or anyone else at the table. But none of her new friends ever relaxed while they were there. The men constantly glared and growled, and the women constantly tried to calm their mates.

Except Peyton. Peyton hadn't stopped glaring at them with bright blue eyes since they'd walked through the door.

"You okay?" Charlie asked Peyton.

Finally, Peyton turned her eyes away and blinked at Charlie. "You're not scared."

Whoa. There was a whole lot of growl in her words. It felt like her wolf had taken over without taking her skin.

"No. I think I'm too drunk to be scared," Charlie admitted with a shrug.

"Good. Stay that way."

"Peyton has a psychotic wolf inside of her. If she thinks a woman or child is at risk, the wolf goes bat shit crazy and tears through anyone or anything it feels is a threat. Hence the reason we call it Cujo," Emory explained.

"I thought Cujo was a rabid dog in a book," Charlie said with a confused frown.

"And movie," Callie said. "And her wolf isn't rabid. Just crazy and terrifying."

"Should've seen when her wolf officially met Callie," Emory said with a fake tremble.

Charlie chuckled.

Then burped.

Loudly.

"Nice," Mason said from across the table.

Aron's eyes darted up to his Pride brother's face and his eyes flared brighter.

"Oh, come on. I'm not flirting with her," Mason said, holding his hands up much like the crows had earlier.

"You guys got to get over that shit," Campbell said as she lifted her empty beer toward Noah. "Can we get another bucket?"

"I got it," Hollyn said, filling it with ice and a bunch of beers.

"I don't think I can drink anymore. My belly is sloshing," Charlie admitted.

"Ready to go home?" Aron asked. He looked so intense as he stared down into her face.

"Are you mad at me?" Charlie asked.

"What? Why would you think that?"

"You look pissed."

Eli, Emory's mate and lion Shifter, leaned forward. "He is. But not at you." His eyes lifted to the crows behind her.

Charlie glanced over at them. Those buttholes were still staring at her. Not all the women now, but only her.

Oh, if only Charlie could growl like the rest of the Shifters. If she tried now, it would sound like a frustrated woman and wouldn't get her point across that they were pushing it. It was definitely time to leave. They should all probably leave as long as the crows were there. It was evident they were trying their damnedest to get under everyone's skin. And by the tension pouring from every single male, it was working.

"Let's go," Charlie said, taking Aron's hand and standing.

Aron rose, as did the rest of the table.

"Can we take these home?" Daxon asked Noah, pointing to the beers left in the bucket.

Noah waved his hand with a grunt, giving him the go ahead.

"Aw. Is the little pussy cat running away?" Clint said.

"Why don't you shut up? We're leaving and you're still trying to start trouble," Charlie said.

"I really like her," Emory said from her left.

"Why don't *you* shut the fuck up, bitch? This has got nothing to do with you. These people even tell you what they are?"

Aron was a blur as he rushed the room, wrapped his big hand around Clint's throat, and lifted him out of the chair.

"What did you call her?" he growled.

The rest of the crows lunged to their feet. Then the members of Big River, Ravenwood, and Blackwater were there, making sure Clint's friends didn't jump Aron.

And all Charlie could do was watch. Her magic was still swimming in the booze she'd consumed. Peyton was slowly stalking forward, her fingernails now Shifted into claws.

"Peyton," her mate, Tristan, warned, wrapping a hand around her bicep and pulling her back. "Everyone's…fine. Stop."

"Aron, let him go. Please. Let's just leave."

"He needs to apologize," Aron growled. As in, he growled every single word.

His panther was so close to the surface.

Noah rounded the bar and put a hand on Aron's shoulder. "Drop him, brother. He ain't worth it."

Aron's eyes flicked to Noah's face then back to Clint. "Talk to her like that again and I'll rip your arm off and beat you with it, fucker."

He dropped Clint hard enough he fell over the side of the chair. But Clint rebounded quickly, jumping to his feet and getting in Aron's face.

"You know what they call a bunch of crows? A murder. Because we're bad news, asshole," Clint said even as he rubbed the marks growing darker on his throat.

"Get the fuck out before I let him kick your ass," Noah grumbled, putting a hand on each man's chest to push them apart.

"He fucks with me and you're kicking me out?"

"Yep. Bye," Noah said, shoving him hard enough to make Clint take a step back.

"Fuck you," Clint said. He stared Aron down a few more seconds and then backed away.

Everyone remained standing as the crows left, taunting and flipping the bird over their shoulder until the door closed behind them.

"Well," Emory said as she retook her seat, "that was fun."

"Why can't we have one night without bull shit," her mate, Eli, said, wrapping an arm around her shoulder and pulling her close.

"I still want to go home," Charlie said. She'd said she wouldn't puke from the alcohol, but she was feeling sick for a whole new reason. The adrenaline was wearing off quickly and sending a chill through her body.

Aron turned to face her. That same intense look was on his face, but his eyes were softer. "I'm sorry," he muttered.

He wrapped his arms around her and brought her hard against his chest. So hard the air left her lungs in a huff.

"What are you sorry for?" she asked, winding her arms around his back and resting her cheek on his chest.

"That shouldn't have happened."

"Okay. But why are you sorry? It had nothing to do with you."

He pulled back enough to look down into her eyes. "I acted like an ass."

Charlie's brows dropped. "Uh, no. *They* acted like asses," she said, jerking her head toward the closed door. "You were simply being a normal person reacting to said asses."

"I seriously like her," Emory said.

Someone chuckled.

"We'll see you guys later," Aron said, laying one arm across Charlie's shoulders.

"Why don't you guys stay at the trailer tonight?" Daxon said. His eyes were still bright. In fact, all the men's eyes still glowed with that pretty iridescent glow.

"Why?" Aron asked.

"Clint was pissed."

"And?"

"If he decides to come looking for you, it'll be the two of you. And you know damn well Clint ain't coming alone. He's too big of a pussy. He'll bring the whole damn Crew."

Aron looked down at Charlie, a question in his eyes.

She'd much rather be alone with Aron in her house. But Daxon was right. If those guys were able to locate her house, it would be him against who knew how many males. Even if they were Shifted, enough crows could hurt Aron's panther. And until the alcohol was out of her system, she wouldn't be much help.

She nodded.

"Let me get her home to pack some clothes. Meet you guys there," he said.

And then they headed to her little house nestled in the woods.

Would her home ever feel like the refuge it had before the rogues had shattered her sense of security?

As she watched Aron's face brighten with the headlights from passing cars, she knew the answer. Yes. Already, she felt stronger. And all it had taken was Aron believing her and pushing her out of her bubble.

****

Aron had never felt so out of control of himself or his animal. At least he'd kept his skin. But only barely.

"I'm sorry," he repeated. Didn't matter how many times she told him it wasn't his fault. He should've kept his cool instead of grabbing Clint the way he had.

Now, that asshole would be gunning for him. He wasn't afraid of the piece of shit, but he didn't want to fight around Charlie. And he sure as fuck didn't want the crows coming onto Charlie's property. For any reason.

She'd come out of her shell so much the last few days. And he knew a large part of that was being around his friends. There was no way anyone could hang out with Reed or Nova or Emory or see the little girls down in Big River territory and think all Shifters were bad or scary.

And then Black Feather Crew had come storming into her life.

But she'd held her own. Even offered to use her magic to make them leave.

That was the last thing he wanted. He didn't want anyone to know about her lineage or her magic. It had been hard enough when someone had discovered what Hollyn was. There was no doubt in his mind the same thing would happen to Charlie.

And he'd burn the fucking planet down before he let anyone touch his mate.

"Stop apologizing," Charlie said.

She undid her seat belt, scooted closer until she was pressed against his side, then buckled the center buckle. Wrapping her hand around his, she pulled it from his thigh and rested on hers, then leaned her head on his shoulder.

"I had fun tonight. Don't let those jerks ruin it," she said around a long, wide yawn.

"I shouldn't have kept you out so late."

"Oh please. I was the one who asked to stay so I could hang out with my cousin. Thank you, by the way."

"You never have to thank me for doing something that makes you happy."

Aron leaned over and pressed a kiss to the top of her head. She smelled like whatever shampoo she'd used late this morning and her unique scent. He could bury his face in her neck and inhale her scent for the rest of his life.

How the hell had he gotten so lucky? He'd never thought of himself as mate material. And he sure as hell never pictured himself with someone so beautiful and strong. And definitely never imagined his mate would be a Fairy.

Yet here he was, falling harder every day for the woman snuggled against his side.

****

Aron pulled onto Charlie's driveway and up to her house, the light from his headlights shining bright across the front. If she'd known they were going to stay out so late she would've left some lights on inside.

But Aron was with her. Even if she couldn't see anyone skulking around inside or in the woods surrounding her property, Aron would smell it if anyone was there.

It only took Charlie a few minutes to pack a couple of changes of clothes. She didn't plan to stay at the panthers' house forever, but she wanted to make sure she had what she'd need in case it ended up being more than a couple of days.

And it was getting cooler out. The panthers always tended to wear t-shirts or long-sleeved t-shirts, even when the temps dropped. Nope. Not Charlie. She needed to be cozy. That meant her oversized sweater got dropped into her pretty pink suitcase.

"I thought everyone used duffel bags these days," Aron said as he carried her stuff to the truck.

"Nah. I like the way it makes me feel when I use a suitcase. Like I'm some fancy lady on my way to an opulent hotel or something."

Yep. Still tipsy. Not only were her words still slurred, so were her thoughts.

"I'll take you to one of those someday," he said as he held his hand out to help her into her seat.

Charlie watched Aron round the hood, her eyes devouring him, and found herself wanting to stay home. She wasn't much of a voyeur so the thought of making love where someone could hear them wasn't exactly appealing.

She could wait a night. If it went past a night, they'd have to either head back to her house or take advantage of any second the other Pride members were out.

When had she become so…insatiable? Duh. When she'd felt every inch of Aron. He was not only an awesome lover, but unselfish. He'd spent so much time making sure she was taken care of before chasing his own release.

"What are you thinking about?" Aron asked, glancing down at her before returning his attention to the road.

"Why?"

"Your scent changed."

And just like that, ice water had been tossed over her head. He could smell her arousal? How embarrassing.

Oh no. Did that mean all the Shifters would know when she was turned on?

That thought did more to sober her then any cup of coffee ever could.

"Charlie?"

"What?" she answered a little too quickly and loudly.

"What were you thinking about?"

Lie. She should lie. Then again, he'd probably know she was lying. Ugh. She needed to avoid drinking from now on. Apparently, she lost her wits when she got drunk.

"You. Us."

"That changed you scent?"

Growling in frustration, Charlie covered her face with both hands. "I was thinking about sex. And how we won't be able to make love as long as we stay in your territory."

Aron didn't say a word as he slowed the truck to a stop at a light. When he turned to her, that iridescent glow was back.

"We're definitely making love when we're in my territory. And again when we're back at your house. I plan on making love to you as often as I can for the rest of my life."

Aaaaand her body was warm again. But so was her heart. He was already picturing their life in the future.

"Do you think we're moving too fast?" she asked, looking up into his face while they waited for the light to change.

"What do you mean?"

"We fell in love within days of admitting we were attracted to each other."

"We're not humans, Charlie. Our bodies, our hearts, and minds don't work the same. And I'm pretty sure I was falling in love with you since the day I saw you throwing those Shifters around the woods."

Charlie couldn't stop staring at Aron's profile as he drove them to Ravenwood territory and parked beside other trucks and an old car.

And then she got a look at the place where she'd be staying a couple of nights.

Daxon had said trailer. So, she assumed it would be a double wide mobile home like the ones she'd seen around town.

Nope. It was a single wide, run down trailer. She'd be surprised if there weren't holes in both the floor and ceiling.

"There are no mice or bugs in there, right?" she asked. She felt mildly guilty asking that about where he lived, but she wasn't used to this kind of place.

A deep chuckle rattled up from his chest. "We're panthers. Cats. Do you really think there'd be any mice?"

Charlie couldn't help the smile that grew on her face. He was so dang funny. In the weeks he'd checked on her, she never would've thought he was so sweet and witty. He'd always been so quiet, so careful about touching her or maintaining eye contact too long.

Now her memory made him feel like two different men.

Campbell stepped out onto the porch as Charlie and Aron neared the front porch.

"Everything good?" she asked. But she wasn't asking Charlie. Her eyes were on Aron.

"Didn't scent anyone."

Campbell nodded, then turned a smile on Charlie. "I'm not usually into girl shit and slumber parties, but I'm super excited to have a little more estrogen around."

"You and Brax live here, too?"

"Nah," Campbell said, wrapping an arm around Charlie's shoulders and taking her from Aron as she led her inside. "I have my own place. It's easier to stay here after hunting late, though."

"You guys didn't hunt tonight," Charlie said, her eyes scanning the room.

While the outside looked like the prop of some horror movie, the inside was relatively nice. Most of the appliances as well as the carpet were outdated. But it was clean and smelled nice inside.

"Yeah, but I knew you were coming over. Like I said, it's nice to be around a little estrogen. It's great hanging out with the female Shifters, but I don't get to see them nearly enough."

Sadness touched Campbell's eyes for a brief second, then was gone. She was sad she didn't get to see the females of the Pack and Clan enough?

Campbell led Charlie through the house, pointing out the different rooms and the bathroom. "Only one," she said with a roll of the eyes. "But the guys tend to pee outside, so it's open more often than not."

The thought of the guys whipping out their junk and peeing off the porch ran through Charlie's alcohol riddled mind and tore a giggle from her lips.

"Are you laughing about them peeing outside?"

"I pictured them all lined up, whipping their things out, and peeing off the porch," Charlie said. Her giggles grew until she was wheezing with laughter.

"I'd prefer you not picture anyone else's junk," Aron said with a shake of his head. But Charlie could tell he was amused by the tiny smile at the corners of his lips.

It was late, but Charlie was still wound up from all the beer and shots, then the drama the crows started. There was no way she would be able to fall asleep anytime soon.

"You guys want to watch a movie? Or play a board game?" Charlie asked, shoving her hands in her back pockets.

"If you're worried about sleeping, you're in a house full of Shifters. Oh, and me. We all know I'm scarier," Campbell joked.

"No. It's not that. I think I'm still full of adrenaline from earlier. I don't want to lie in bed and stare at the ceiling all night."

Aron leaned in, his lips against her ear, his warm breath against her skin. "I can give you something to stare at," he said in the softest whisper.

"You realize we can still hear you," Mason said without pulling his eyes from the video game he was playing.

Heat once again rushed Charlie's cheeks. "You guys keep making me blush," she blurted out.

"Do you want to take a shower or anything before bed?" Campbell asked.

"Let me take care of my mate, damn it," Aron said.

Campbell held her hands up but grinned.

"Do you want to take a shower?" Aron asked, repeating the same thing Campbell had asked.

Charlie smiled and patted Aron on the cheek. "Actually, yeah. People were smoking at the bar and I don't want to get in your bed smelling like an ashtray." And then something hit her. "Wait. *Am* I sleeping in your bed? I mean, I can sleep on the couch if you want."

"You're not sleeping out here without me. You can take my bed and I'll take the floor."

"You already tried that at my house. It didn't work."

"You slept on her floor?" Mason asked, turning and looking at them over the back of the couch.

"He slept outside my door the first night. Then on my floor last night."

Campbell tilted her head. "It seriously feels like you two have spent more than two nights together."

"Probably from all the nights Aron spent checking her property while slept. Ow! What the hell?" Mason said after Aron slapped in on the back of the head.

"Shut…up," Aron said.

Mason glanced at him, then did a double take. "Dude. Are you blushing? Is our strong, wise, mysterious leader actually blushing?"

"Jackass," Aron muttered.

He took Charlie's hand and led her down the hall to the one bathroom. Grabbing a towel from a closet behind the door, he placed it on the sink, then pointed out the shampoo and soap.

Campbell yelled from the living room, "You can use my stuff. You don't want to smell like a dude."

"Thanks!" Charlie yelled back.

Charlie quickly showered and washed her hair. She didn't see a blow dryer anywhere, so she braided her long hair and twisted a rubber band she'd found on the back of the toilet around the end.

Aron was standing outside of the bathroom, leaning against the wall, his arms crossed over his chest. For a second, she'd thought he had waited out there while she showered. Then she noticed he wore a pair of gray sweatpants and no shirt.

Holy hell. How was she supposed to keep her hands to herself and her hormones under control when he looked so damn good?

"You waited for me?"

"Just happened to step out of the room when I heard you coming out," Aron said.

"He waited," Mason said.

"Dude. Shut up!" Aron said, but there was zero force behind it.

Seeing him like this with his Pride showed Charlie a whole new side of Aron. He might have been the Alpha of Ravenwood, but he was just a…guy. He wasn't some Shifter or badass in this place. He was just Aron.

"You ready for bed?"

A long yawn escaped her lips before she had the chance to hold it in. Guess the adrenaline was finally wearing off. Or it could've been the hot shower. Either way, she felt her eyelids growing heavy. She wasn't sure she'd have the energy to make love even if they were alone.

Aron escorted her down the short hall and to a bedroom on the left. His room was tidy save for the unmade bed and dirty shirt on the floor next to the hamper. She never could understand why men didn't simply put the clothes *inside* the hamper.

His bed was barely a queen. It might have even been a double. It looked smaller than hers and she wondered if he would fit on it without his feet hanging off the end.

"I don't want you to sleep on the floor," Charlie said, turning to face him once he'd closed the door.

"Charlie–"

"No. Nope. No arguing. We're both dressed. There are too many people for me to be comfortable having sex without every single one of them hearing every noise I make. And I want you to hold me. I want your arms wrapped around me as I drift off to sleep."

Aron huffed out a sigh and dropped his head. "I'm not going to win this one, am I?" he said, lifting only his eyes to look at her.

Charlie shook her head and tried to hide her smile.

"Fine." He led her to his bed, pulled the blanket back, and waited for her to climb in. He rounded the end, then climbed up the mattress since the room was so small the bed was butted up against the wall.

"Doesn't that creep you out?"

"What?" he said, yawning as wide and long as she had minutes ago.

"Being so close to the outer wall. I used to convince myself a monster could break through and grab me when I was a kid."

"I am the monster," he muttered, his eyes closed.

"Goodnight, Aron," she whispered, snuggling against his side and smiling when he hugged her closer.

"Goodnight, sweetheart."

Chapter Eight

Charlie had slept in Aron's bed the last three nights.

And they hadn't made love since.

He had tried to assure her no one would be paying attention to what they did in his room, but Mason and Campbell constantly teased her. Therefore, they were in a dry spell.

Okay. Three days wasn't exactly a dry spell, but now that he'd felt her warmth wrapped around his cock, he knew he'd never get enough of her. He knew he'd never get tired of her. Of waking up beside her. Of hearing her voice. Of feeling her warm tightness.

Even as he showered and got ready to drop her off in Big River territory so he could work for a few hours with the bears, his junk was hard and achy. He couldn't remember the last time he walked around in a constant state of arousal.

He felt like a damned teenage boy.

"You sure I can't go home until you get off work?" she asked as she tugged on a pair of boots.

"I don't trust the crows. I fucked up by attacking Clint. He won't let that shit go. I don't want him fucking with you to get to me. You've been through enough."

"Hey, as long as I'm sober, I can use my wind."

Aron pulled her close and kissed her forehead. "I know you can take care of yourself. Consider it a favor to me so I won't be worried about you all day."

Charlie sighed theatrically. "Fine," she said it as if he'd put her out.

All the women from Big River were present as Aron pulled his truck up the long dirt driveway leading to the wolves' territory. Even some of the lionesses from Hope Pride up the hill were there. Which kind of surprised Aron.

The women had all come from shitty Prides. Some had been one of several mates to a single male. They'd been mistreated and disrespected their entire lives, sometimes even being sold off or given away by their own families.

Eli and Emory had started Hope Pride to give the women the freedom they deserved. They took in any female who needed to escape. And Eli and the wolves provided a sense of security.

But they were still leery of strangers. Especially men. The fact they'd come down to hang with Charlie said a lot about her sweet disposition. There was no way anyone could be around her and not fall in love with her.

He should know.

"Hey girl," Nova said, little Rieka on her hip. "Say hi to Charlie," she told the toddler.

"Hi, Tawley," the little girl said.

Reed and Lola's daughter, Grace, was only barely making sounds that sounded like words lately.

"Hi, sweetie," Charlie said, moving closer to tickle the toddler's chubby belly.

"Is Campbell coming?" Lola asked as she set Grace in the playpen in the middle of the circle of chairs.

"I think so. Why?" Aron asked.

"The girls have been wanting to play with Polo," Nova said with a wide grin. She lowered her little girl to her feet and smiled as she waddled over to where Grace played.

"In?" she asked Lola, who lifted her inside the playpen to play with her little friend.

Aron pulled his phone out and texted the human member of Ravenwood, asking her to bring her large dog for the girls.

After a few seconds, she replied with a thumbs up emoji.

"She's bringing him," Aron told Lola.

"You ready for a day without so much testosterone?" Peyton asked Charlie, taking her by the arm to lead her over to the where the rest of the women waited.

"Hey, Charlie," Callie said, patting an empty chair beside her.

"You going to be okay all day?" Aron asked her.

"Nah. We planned on drugging her, stripping off her bra, and freezing it while she slept. You might want to stick around. Just in case," Nova teased him.

Aron shot her a smile then dropped his eyes. Then thought, what the hell? Raising his gaze back to Nova's face, he smiled wide and he let a little chuckle escape. "Try to make sure she's dressed before I get back," he said.

Nova slapped a hand to her chest in feigned shock. "He spoke to me!" she said, turning to look at the rest of the women. "Did you see that? The big, bad panther Shifter actually spoke to me. And looked at me."

"They're a bad influence," he said, jerking his chin toward his mate, who smiled at him over the top of the lawn chair she'd claimed. "I'll call you later. I love you."

"I love you, too," Charlie called back.

"Awww!" Nova and Emory said in unison. "They're so cute," Nova said.

Aron could only imagine the conversation after he'd left. Nova was always trying to get the details of everyone's sex life. She always said it was inspiration for her books. Aron sometimes wondered if she wasn't simply a perv.

****

Charlie couldn't remember the last time she'd laughed so much in her life. Nova and Emory were hilarious. Callie was so sweet and gentle. Lola and Peyton laughed along with Charlie and threw in a few jokes and teases here and there, too.

And of course, Campbell was super popular when she showed up with her big Rottweiler, Polo. The dog was enormous and looked intimidating as heck. But he was so gentle with the little girls and seemed to love the attention they gave him.

The women from the Pride from the top of the hill connected to Big River territory were quiet, but they were sweet, too. They'd talk to her, but only if she started the conversation. Except for a female named Luna. Turned out she was Emory's sister-in-law of sorts. Luna talked to all of them and was at ease around everyone.

"So," Nova started, waggling her brows up and down at Charlie.

"Oh no," Emory said with a smile and a shake of her head. "Watch out, Charlie. She's about to ask a lot of personal questions."

"About what?" Charlie said, looking from one woman to the other.

"About your sex life," Peyton answered. She lifted her arms and wound a ponytail holder around her hair, pulling it back and out of her face and revealing quite a bit of bright purple hair underneath.

"And she'll use anything you tell her in a book. Trust me." She cocked one brow and shot an irritated look Nova's way.

"Ew. No way. Don't use me in a book."

"It won't be you, per se," Nova said, waving off Charlie's protest.

"How many books have you written?" Charlie asked.

"Man. I don't actually know. I stopped counting around sixty."

"Holy cow!" Charlie said, looking around the circle to gauge their reactions. No one else batted an eye. They were used to Nova's profession.

"I make a lot of money. A *lot*," Nova said. "But these jerks never let me buy them anything."

"Wait," Charlie said, glancing behind her at the row of tiny homes. "If you make so much money, why do you live…like that?"

Nova shrugged. "I figure it's no different than living in an apartment. And I get to be close to my family this way. Besides, the only time we spend in the house is when we're sleeping, eating, showering, or making love."

"And here comes the TMI," Peyton said.

The little girls came tearing through the center of the chairs squealing and giggling as Polo trotted behind them, his nub of a tail wagging like crazy.

"He sure does love those girls," Campbell said, smiling as her dog continued to follow Rieka and Grace around.

"That's so confusing. I was always told animals don't like Shifters. We always had a dog when we were growing up as a security alarm," Charlie said, turning to watch the girls and Polo.

"They usually don't. My cat freaked out anytime Tristan used to come around. And it took him forever to become my baby again after I got Turned," Peyton said. "Mr. Darcy won't come near anyone else, though."

"Are there any other pets here?" Charlie asked.

"Nope. Unless you count those two monsters," Lola said, pointing to her daughter and Rieka.

Conversation slowed, and Charlie realized the pregnant lioness from Blackwater was missing. Actually, she hadn't really met the other women from the Clan, either.

"Do the bears' mates not come out much?" Charlie asked.

"With Shawnee pregnant, everyone's been trying to stick close to home to keep her safe. She can't Shift to protect herself if anything were to happen. And she's super close to giving birth. And you know Hollyn works the bar with Noah almost every day. You'll meet June and Piper eventually," Emory said. "Speaking of, I've got to get ready for work."

"Where do you work?" Charlie asked.

"A feed store down in House Springs. It's right across the street from Moe's."

"Any chance they're hiring?"

Emory's brows shot up to her forehead. "You're looking for a job?"

"I don't really *have* to work," Charlie explained. "But now that I have all you guys, I feel weird not doing something. You know? You all have these cool lives and a purpose. I want that."

"You're purpose in life is to keep Aron happy," Nova teased. "That and stay bestest friends with us forever and ever."

Everyone chuckled at Nova's silliness. The smile fell off Nova's face so fast her ears moved.

"Wait. Why don't you have to work? Are you a top-secret author, too?"

"Ha! No. I couldn't write a book if my life depended on it. No. My family were always really good at investing and all that stuff. When they were…" Charlie inhaled deeply as the familiar sting of grief squeezed her heart. "When they all died, it was all left to me. That's how I've been able to move around so much to avoid being found by Shifters."

No one spoke.

Shoot. That sounded bad. And she'd more than likely hurt their feelings.

"I mean…"

"It's fine, honey," Callie said, reaching over to pat her hand. "We get it. You're sitting with a group of females who had to fight for freedom from males. We know how it feels to have to hide from people who'd take advantage of you or hurt you."

"I hope you all don't think I see you that way. I really don't. You're all the first Shifters I've ever really known. And you're all so nice."

"Seriously," Peyton said, leaning forward. "It's fine. I wasn't born this way. An asshole Shifter put the wolf inside of me. Just like humans, and I guess Fairies, there are good and bad everywhere."

"Yeah. There are bad Fairies," Campbell said. "One was trying to sell off Hollyn. She's the reason Hollyn came to live here in the first place."

"Really? I knew Hollyn had been targeted by the rogues, but she didn't tell me a fellow Fae had anything to do with it. That's terrifying."

"Not just a Fairy. A female, at that. She was helping the rogues track down other Fae to sell for higher pay," Campbell explained. "There was a big fight, according to Brax."

"Yep. The wolves, bears, and even Brax and Daxon were in that one," Emory said. "Hollyn used her fire and kicked some ass."

The day was a little uncomfortable after that. She knew one hundred percent none of these people were a risk to her. But the thought of a female Fairy turning on her own kind made Charlie sick to her stomach.

How many women like that were out there? She'd seen the human news where women were responsible for trafficking other women and children, and she'd never understood. Didn't they ever think about how they'd feel if that happened to them or someone they loved?

Obviously not. People like that didn't tend to have too much empathy or compassion.

By the time Aron came back, she'd learned so much about the women. She'd learned about how Eli had more or less stalked the property because his lion needed to watch over Emory. She'd learned how Nova had come to Big River for protection when the Shifter Council had discovered she'd been writing Shifter romance under her real name. She'd learned the reason they had a fancy new firepit was because Callie had come crashing into the last one when she ran from the male who was trying to force her into a pairing.

She'd learned every single one of these women had had a shitty past but overcame it and became stronger.

"Did you have fun?" Aron asked as he drove them back to Ravenwood territory.

"I did. Thanks for making me go," she said, turning to look at him.

"I didn't technically make you go. I requested you stay with them for my own sanity."

"Tomato. Tomahto."

He snorted a laugh and shook his head.

"I learned a lot about them. And about myself," she said as she turned to watch the trees pass by. It was so pretty here this time of year with all the golds and oranges and reds.

"What do you mean?"

Charlie looked at his profile. "They had a crappy history, too. But they didn't let it affect their futures. They didn't lose sleep or drop a bunch of weight."

"They might have in the beginning. Callie was pretty shy when she went to Big River. And you see how the lionesses are. Everyone deals with trauma differently."

Charlie shrugged even though Aron wasn't looking at her. "All I know is I won't let a group of jerk wads affect me anymore. I can't stop my body from reacting, but I can make sure I don't mentally dwell anymore. And I refuse to be scared of them." She inhaled deeply and let it out in a rush. "I definitely want to start hunting with you guys. I don't expect you to treat me like Campbell. I can't fight like her. But I can be back up for you guys. I can do like Mason did and stay with the car for a quick getaway. Or I can use my magic to make sure no one sneaks up behind any of you. I promise, I won't get in the way and I won't let anyone hurt me again."

Aron watched her for so long she opened her mouth to tell him to watch the road.

When he finally turned his eyes away, a muscle ticked in his jaw.

"Can we talk about this?" There was a growl lacing his words. And she knew it wasn't anger; it was fear for his mate.

She knew the feeling. Even before they'd admitted their feelings to each other, she used to lie in bed and wonder if he was okay. She'd known then he was still out there hunting the rogues and saving more women like herself. She'd feared for his safety before they were mates.

And now, she feared for his safety even more.

"We've already talked about it. I know you're worried. I promise, I pinky swear I'll be okay."

The corners of his lips twitched. "Pinky swear, huh?"

Charlie held her left pinky up and offered it to Aron.

With a chuckle, he switched hands on the wheel so he could wrap his right pinky around hers.

"Deal. So…can we go tonight?" she asked, pulling her hand from his.

"I want Campbell to teach you a few things first. And I want you to learn how to use a gun."

"Why would I need a gun? You saw what I can do with my magic."

"It's another of those things that will make me feel better," he said, glancing at her once before turning onto their driveway.

****

Aron had procrastinated as long as he could. He'd made excuse after excuse, asking Campbell for more training for Charlie every day after they'd finish the last round. But his mate wasn't stupid. She'd caught on after the second day.

They were now on day five and she stood in the living room, her arms crossed over her chest as she glared at Aron.

"I know how to use a gun. I know how to get out of a hold. I know how to throw a punch. I'm ready, Aron."

The rest of Ravenwood sat silently listening to the fight, their eyes bouncing back and forth as they listened to each person.

"A couple more days. The rogues will still be there in a couple of days."

"Yeah. And how many women will go missing in that time, Aron? No one has hunted in five days because they've all been working with me."

The entire Pride had stuck around to help. No one else had actually touched her or demonstrated any moves. But they made suggestions based on Charlie's small height and cheered her on.

"I think she's ready," Campbell said.

"I agree," Brax said.

"Me, too." Daxon.

"Me, three." Mason, of course.

"You aren't helping," Aron said, jabbing a finger at his Pride.

The problem was he wasn't *Charlie's* Alpha. She didn't have to follow his orders. Not that he'd ever order her around.

But in this instance, he sure as fuck wished he could. He'd order her to stay with Big River each time they went out to track down more traffickers.

"One more night of training," he bargained.

"No." She remained in the same position, her arms crossed, her chin jutted out. She was ready to take him on no matter what excuse he came up with.

"We'll keep her close, Aron," Mason said, shoving his feet in his boots.

"I'll keep her with me. This one doesn't let me jump in first, anyway," Campbell said, jerking her head toward her mate, Brax.

"Damn it. Y'all aren't helping!"

"We're not trying to help you. I'm totally siding with my girl on this one," Campbell said, smiling at Charlie.

Aron weighed every pro and con in his head. The last thing he wanted to do was piss off his mate, but he hated the thought of her out there with those assholes. It would take one swipe of a claw or one bite and he'd lose her. There was no way he'd want to continue on this planet now that he'd found her. Not alone. Not without his Charlie.

"Fine. But you stay with Campbell. And you both stay behind us," Aron said. He was fully aware how much of his panther was in his words. And he'd bet his left nut his eyes were glowing.

"Awesome. Let me change," Charlie said, her mood instantly lifting as she jogged toward the bedroom they'd shared for the last two weeks.

He hadn't heard a word from Black Feather, but that didn't mean they weren't holding a grudge. Eventually, though, Charlie would want to return to her home. And he'd take her. He'd make sure to stay with her or walk the perimeter every night.

Chapter Nine

Charlie was damned near bouncing in her seat. She was officially hunting with Ravenwood. She was hunting with the panthers and Campbell. And the entire Pride trusted her abilities were an asset.

So why were nerves turning her stomach? It was a mixture of anxiety and fear as well as a hefty amount of vengeance, if that was even an emotion. If it wasn't, it sure as hell should be.

She would finally have a purpose for her life. She could protect other women. Prevent other families from the grief of losing a daughter, sister, mother, or granddaughter.

"Hey," she said as Mason drove the car and Aron sat in the back with her.

"Yeah?" Aron said. He didn't look at her. His focus was on the area as they kept the windows rolled down to pick up the scent of any Shifters or humans.

"Does this mean I'm a Ravenwood Pride member now? Since I'm hunting with you?"

Daxon glanced back at her from the front seat while Aron looked down at her from beside her.

Daxon's grin was wide. "You were a Ravenwood member the second you agreed to be mate to our Alpha," he said.

"You've been a member, honey," Aron said.

Campbell patted her on the shoulder. "You're stuck with us, sister."

"Ooooh. Now I have two sisters," Mason said from the driver's seat.

"You're a dork," Campbell said from behind him.

They drove for close to an hour before Mason held a hand up and pointed toward a thick press of trees that climbed for what seemed like forever. Were there mountains in Missouri? She didn't remember ever reading about any, but that sure looked like one from where they parked on the side of the road.

"Bingo," Daxon said, pushing his door open.

Charlie moved to push her own door open, but Aron wrapped a hand around her bicep, halting her. "Any way I can convince you to wait at the car?"

"I thought Mason did that."

"He does. Did. But if you stayed back, you could have the SUV ready to roll if we come down with a victim."

"She'll be alone," Campbell muttered, almost like she was intentionally saying it so Charlie wouldn't hear it.

But she did.

"Yeah. You don't want me down here alone, do you?"

Aron's face darkened. He knew both females were right, though.

"Damn it," he ground out between clenched teeth. "Stay with Campbell. You both stay behind us." He turned to look at Campbell. "That means no running off to flank the rogues. Got it? 'Cause she'll follow you."

"She'll be fine," Brax said as he scooted out behind his mate.

Aron took Charlie's face in both hands, dipped his head, and pressed his lips to hers in a desperate kiss. He didn't deepen it, rather held her there for a few seconds before pulling back. "Please be careful."

"I've got this, Aron. Trust me. Trust my magic."

As long as her wind didn't go MIA like it had that night at Moe's, she'd be okay. But she hadn't had a drink since that day. Everything should be fine.

Daxon, Brax, and Campbell waited for Aron and Charlie at the start of the trees. It was dark and Charlie didn't quite have the keen eyesight of the Shifters, but neither did Campbell. The full moon over their heads was a saving grace as the women followed the guys silently, doing their best to avoid crunching leaves or twigs.

After a few minutes, she caught the sound of men laughing and a female whimpering and begging them to let her go. Those sounds fueled the rage inside of Charlie until her wind swelled and spilled out a little.

Campbell's hair rustled, and she looked back at Charlie with a question in her eyes. Charlie shrugged and mouthed 'sorry.' She didn't dare speak out loud. The Shifters would hear her and know someone was coming to break up their party.

When she had been taken, there had been six males. This time, there were eleven. Six against eleven. Well, five since Mason waited back the SUV.

Five to eleven. Those were not good odds.

Aron looked at Campbell and Charlie and held his hand out, telling them to stop. He looked to Brax and Daxon. They had some kind of silent conversation, stripped their clothes off, then Shifted into their massive panthers. Even in their animal forms, Charlie wondered it this would turn out as anything other than a nightmare.

But she couldn't let those rogues take off with another woman. She had to do whatever she could to stop it.

As she watched, the sound of a bird cried loudly somewhere in the distance. Looking up, she didn't see anything. It was too dark. Didn't matter. She needed her focus on the situation ahead of her. She had to make sure she backed up the panthers with her magic like she'd promised.

Shame they didn't have Hollyn there, too. Between Hollyn and Charlie, they could send a fiery tornado toward the males and burn them to a crisp.

They didn't have Hollyn, though. Charlie had to stay true to her word and stay safe while keeping her Pride safe.

And they were her Pride. Every day, these people felt more and more like family. They treated her as if she'd been there all along, as if she'd been born into the family.

Three, humongous black panthers stretched, and then checked on the women once more. This was only the second time Charlie had seen Aron's panther.

He was magnificent.

She knew without a doubt she would know him out of a hundred panthers. His eyes spoke to her without a single word being said. He pled with her to stay behind him, to stay safe. He told her how he felt about her, how much he loved her.

Smiling softly, she nodded once, letting him know she understood.

And then the panthers charged forward with Campbell and Charlie running behind them at human – or humanish – speeds.

The ten males turned, startled, and three of them immediately Shifted into their wolf forms. Two men grabbed the dark-haired woman and tried to drag her away and into the woods.

Not a chance would Charlie allow that to happen.

Raising her hands, she smiled as her hair blew back from her face. Her wind was ready for action.

She threw both hands out, aiming carefully at the males. They were ripped away from the woman and thrown further into the woods until she could no longer see them.

"Hurry!" Campbell yelled to the woman. "We're here to help. Run this way."

Campbell and Charlie were making their way forward, but the woman was frozen in place.

Charlie winced when one of the guys actually swung at Campbell. She ducked and swung her own fist, making contact with his nose with a sickening crunch. She followed it with a round house kick, knocking him off his feet.

Then she pulled her firearm from its holster on her hip.

Charlie checked on the panthers. All three fought against multiple wolves at a time. More men had Shifted. There were now seven wolves. Two males were still missing, still somewhere in the woods. And the guy Campbell had knocked down was climbing back to his feet.

"Shit," Campbell said, aiming her gun at the melee in front of her.

Two wolves were on Brax and Daxon, three were on Aron.

Not on her watch. She wouldn't let anyone hurt her mate or her new family.

As Charlie's hair whipped in a frenzy, the ends slapping her in the face, she directed as much as she could at the wolf on Aron's back, careful to avoid pushing Aron with the force.

The wolf flew against a tree with enough force to cause several snaps and cracks. The wolf fell to the ground and didn't move.

As she watched the fight, she waited for a moment, waited for a small gap between the bodies to lift them off any of the panthers. They were too close together. If she thrust her wind forward, she'd throw one of the panthers.

"Shit. Shit shit shit," Campbell said, still aiming her firearm.

And then Campbell ran closer. Charlie was supposed to stay back. But she was also told to stay with Campbell.

She was a Ravenwood Pride member.

She wouldn't let them down.

Running behind Campbell, she focused all her energy on the male latching his teeth around Daxon's throat. With one hand, she pointed her full wind at him, pulling him away. And then she cringed; the bastard almost didn't let go. Her move could've cost Daxon his life rather than saved it.

Campbell aimed her gun at the head of one of the wolves and pulled the trigger. He instantly fell to the side of Brax.

Okay. The numbers were dwindling. And Charlie was actually being helpful instead of causing a distraction by her mere presence.

It was now six to five. Much better odds.

Aron finished off a wolf, then went after the one who tried to run away.

And the woman was still frozen in place.

Not bothering to wait for instructions, Charlie rushed forward, grabbed her hand, and pulled her until she was a safer distance from the warring Shifters.

"Take her to Mason," Campbell called as she aimed at another wolf who was on Daxon's back.

These bastards didn't fight fair.

Hand still wrapped around the woman, Charlie took off running, pulling the terrified woman behind her.

The second they were close enough, Charlie yelled, "Mason!"

He darted forward, his eyes wide. "Is everyone okay?"

"Yeah. Take her. I got to go back."

"Do they need me?"

"No. It was almost fair when I left."

Charlie didn't wait for a reply, didn't ask the woman's name. Just took off back up the hill, back to her mate.

By the time she made it up there, the fight was over. All but one wolf was dead. The one still alive laid there panting heavily, then Shifted back into his human form.

The panthers all melted back into their skin, as well, and it took everything Charlie had not to notice all the tallywackers flopping in the air.

Charlie lifted her hands toward the man sitting on his bare ass on the forest floor. "Want me to…"

"No," Aron said, stalking forward. "Want to talk? Or do you want to find out what it feels like to die?"

The guy lifted his eyes to Aron's face. It was only then Charlie realized how young he was. The guy couldn't be more than eighteen or nineteen.

"I didn't have a choice, dude," he said softly.

"What the fuck does that mean?" Daxon asked.

"I didn't have a choice." His voice was even softer. And Charlie's heart broke for the look in his eyes.

The guys exchanged a look. Campbell and Charlie frowned at each other. Charlie moved forward until Aron's hand on her arm stopped her.

"Close enough."

Lowering to her knees, Charlie snagged his attention. "Why didn't you have a choice?"

Birds were crying in the trees somewhere in the distance again. She would've thought the forest would have been asleep except for nocturnal creatures. That didn't matter right now, though. All the mattered was the broken boy in front of her with watery eyes.

****

If anyone could get a person to spill their guts it would be Charlie. He'd noticed early on people gravitated to her. They'd spent years checking on the women they'd saved, but they'd always played paper, scissor, rock over most of them.

Not with Charlie. Everyone wanted to be the one to make sure she was okay.

The boy on the ground raised his head, and Aron felt like a dick when a tear rolled down his cheek. He was literally a boy. A teenager. A kid. What the hell was he doing with the rest of these assholes?

"What's your name?" Charlie asked, her hands rested on her knees. She bent forward to make sure he looked at her.

"James. My sister calls me Jamie."

"Was that your sister?" she asked, pointing to where the girl had been standing while they'd fought.

"No."

"Where's your sister?" Aron asked. He had a feeling where this conversation was going.

"They took her. They want fighters to help them get the women before you guys show up."

"You guys knew we'd come?" Daxon asked, stepping closer.

"You always show up," he said with a sarcastic bark of laughter. "At least that's the way they tell it."

"Who's they? The rogues?" Aron asked.

James opened his mouth to answer until a cacophony of birds squawked in the trees overhead.

All heads lifted to look for the birds but didn't see any.

But Aron had an idea of who it was.

Leaning closer, Aron said, "Are they watching?"

James's eyes darted to the trees then to the ground. And then he didn't say another word.

"Come on." Aron jerked James to his feet and dragged him down the hill with the rest of Ravenwood.

Mason stood outside the SUV while the woman sat in the backseat, her arms wrapped around herself.

"What the fuck is this? Since when do we take prisoners?" Mason asked, his eyes bright as he glared at James.

"He's not a prisoner," Aron said, shaking his head in the slightest movement.

Mason caught it. He snapped his mouth shut and rounded the back of the vehicle to get into the driver's seat.

Daxon let Charlie ride up front while he and Aron flanked James, with Campbell and Brax flanking the woman.

Normally, they'd ask her name. Ask her where she lived. Ask her where she wanted to go. They wouldn't do any of that with James in the car. Not until they determined one hundred percent he wasn't a threat.

They needed to find out if the sister story was true. And if it was, they needed to find out where she was being held. And then they needed to get her free so she could go back to her life.

Aron pulled his phone from his pocket and pulled up Gray's number.

"Hello?" he answered, a mixture of curiosity and concern in his voice.

"I need a favor," Aron said.

"Name it." Gray was a solid dude.

"I've got a situation."

"Are you in danger?"

"Not at the moment," Aron said. He'd rather not talk in front of James, but they needed to get as much space between themselves and the woods as possible. Although, if his gut instinct was right, the threat could very well be following them.

"Do you have anyone in the Council?"

"No. Nova's dad left after Colton's dad was killed and Rieka was born."

Shit. Aron thought maybe he could leave James with some members of the Council while they made sure the woman was safe and wouldn't call the police.

He didn't want to deliver James to Big River or Blackwater territory, though. There were two babies in Big River and Shawnee was ready to pop over in Blackwater.

"You know any other Shifters in the area you'd trust?"

"Yeah. Lola's old Pack. Morse Pack. Her dad is still there and the new Alpha's a good guy."

"Give them a call and see if I can drop off a possible threat."

Gray was quiet a few moments. Then, "You sure you're not in danger? You need us to watch over Charlie and Campbell?"

Solid dude.

"They're fine for now. But thanks for the offer."

"Alright. Give me a few and I'll call you back," Gray said then ended the call without another word.

A few minutes later, he was given the go ahead and directions to Morse Pack territory. It was only about twenty minutes from where they were currently.

The Alpha, Koda, waited outside with a few other males. A couple females waited on porches connected to log homes. The place reminded him of those small-town movies he'd seen as a kid.

"What's the problem?" Koda asked as Aron stepped out of the car.

Aron pulled James from the SUV by his arm and marched him to Koda. "I need you to watch over him for a few while I take his victim home."

Koda's eyes instantly flashed bright blue. "This fucker a rogue?"

"That's a question we're trying to get the answer to. He's got a pretty good story. But listen," Aron said, his eyes going to the sky. "There's a chance we were followed."

Koda followed Aron's line of sight then looked at him again. "Are my females at risk?"

"I don't believe so. But I can't promise you. If it's too much, we'll take him with us."

Koda scratched the stubble on his jaw. "Nah. Leave him here. If there are any problems, we'll call in reinforcements."

Aron didn't ask who those reinforcements were, but knew Morse had a bad reputation at one point years ago. Rumor had it Koda had turned the Pack around and ran it with honor.

"Thanks, brother," Aron said, reaching forward and shaking Koda's hand. "We'll be back as soon as possible."

They had no idea how far this woman had traveled or where she'd been snatched from, but Aron was determined to get her home even if he had to buy her a plane ticket.

Once they were out of ear shot of Morse Pack and James, Aron turned to the woman.

"What's your name, ma'am?"

"Teresa," she answered as her bottom lip quivered.

"You're safe now, Teresa. We're going to get you home. But we ask that you not tell anyone what happened tonight. That includes your friends and family. Or even the police."

"What would I tell them? That I was kidnapped by men who turned into giant wolves who then fought giant panthers? They'd lock me up in the insane asylum." She giggled a little, but it seemed more hysterical rather than out of humor.

She gave Mason her address. It was almost an hour from where they were now. Damn. The rogues were moving all around Missouri for victims. Although he knew there were more than the ones who lived in Jefferson County. Those assholes were all around the world, similar to the human sex traffickers.

Charlie climbed into the backseat with Aron and held Teresa's hand the whole drive. Mason didn't say a word about being alone while he drove them into North St. Louis.

"You're safe," Charlie whispered to Teresa. "These guys saved me, too."

Teresa turned wide eyes to Charlie. "They took you? You got away?"

"Yep. I promise it's scary now. You don't have to think of yourself as a victim, though. You're a survivor, sis."

Aron couldn't be prouder of his mate as she comforted the human. How the hell had he gotten so lucky?

Chapter Ten

Teresa was so sweet. Charlie could tell even through her trauma. It would've been better if they could've spent more time with her, but Aron told Charlie he was suspicious over a few things that happened in the woods.

For one thing, he'd noticed the birds going crazy when they were talking to James, too. Charlie had wondered about that being as it was so late.

And now she knew there was a huge possibility what she'd heard hadn't been some nocturnal animals.

Aron had contacted his friends. A few of them stood around James, their thick arms crossed over their barrel chests. Seriously. Were all of Aron's friends massive? Probably a Shifter thing.

"Everything go okay?" Gray asked when the panthers and Campbell and Charlie stepped from the vehicle.

"Yep," Aron said, clasping Gray's hand in a rough handshake.

He went around and did the same thing with the bears and wolves who had showed up. It wasn't lost on Charlie the only female who came was Peyton. After what she'd learned about the woman, Peyton might be the more ferocious one out of everyone present.

"What's going on?" Luke, one of the bears from Blackwater, asked. His eyes darted down to where James sat on the dirt then back up to Aron. "This piece of shit one of the rogues going after women?"

"I think there's more to it," Charlie answered. When all eyes turned on her, a moment of shyness rushed through her. "I mean, I know you asked Aron, but all you guys look intense and like you want to kill someone."

Even Peyton looked murderous with her bright blue eyes.

"What do you mean there's more?" Luke asked, his expression softer when he questioned her.

Charlie turned to James, who was watching her with a look she couldn't decipher. Anger? Sorrow? Fear? Whichever it was, she needed to make sure they all got the information they needed and kept the young man safe.

She realized as she looked down into his young face that she'd want to protect him even if he turned out to be full of crap. He was a kid. He still had a lot of living and learning to do. Maybe he had fallen in with the wrong crowd or his family were bad guys. With the right people, he could be a good guy.

"They have my sister," James said, his voice breaking on the last syllable.

"*Who* has your sister?" Koda, Alpha of Morse Pack, asked.

James looked around, checking the trees, and confirming Aron's and Charlie's suspicions.

"The crows." His voice was barely a whisper.

Charlie felt like she'd been punched in the stomach as all the air left her body. The crows? The same people they'd seen at Moe's days ago? They were right there and none of them had known a thing.

"Are they capable of something like that?" Peyton asked. "They seemed like assholes, but I wouldn't have thought they would be into kidnapping women."

The world tilted a little as Charlie began to wonder if they'd been there for a different reason. Had they known Charlie would be there? Or were they after Hollyn? She wasn't sure how many in the community were aware Hollyn was a Fairy, but it was totally possible someone had overheard one of her friends. Which was why her kind had always been careful about what they spoke about to whom.

It was awful coincidental the crows happened to be at Moe's when there were two Fae inside.

Keeping those thoughts to herself for now – there was no reason to freak Aron out – Charlie knelt as close to James as Aron would let her get.

"Can you tell us where? Are they working with the rogues?"

Again, James's eyes darted to the trees. "I can't say anything else."

Everyone followed his line of sight. Charlie didn't see anything in the trees. And as far as she could tell, neither did anyone else.

Koda pulled James to his feet roughly, his hand wrapped tightly around a bicep, then dragged him into the closest house.

A female looked up with a frown when the door was opened.

"Can you give us a second?" he asked, dipping his head slightly in a show of respect.

"Sure," the female said, that frown still pulling her brows down as she studied James, looked to Charlie, who had followed, then to the crowd of males standing in the doorway.

Once everyone was inside and the door was closed, Koda pushed James into a chair, then spoke so softly Charlie had to move closer to hear what he said.

"Talk."

James's eyes bounced from person to person. Then they settled on Charlie. He must have felt more comfortable with her since she hadn't shown any animosity or aggression toward him.

"My sister's only sixteen. It's only the two of us. Our parents were killed a year ago."

"I'm so sorry," Charlie said, her hand going to her mouth.

He nodded in jerky movements. "Thank you," he said softly. After a hard swallow, he finished his story. "We didn't have anywhere to go. I met a guy named Clint. He offered us a place to go."

"Mother fucker," Aron growled.

"I thought it was safe. I was responsible for Beth's safety. And then he wanted me to help him and the Talonwood Pack."

"Who the hell is that?" Gray said at the same time Koda said, "Holy shit!"

Everyone turned their attention to Koda.

"You know them?" Gray asked.

"Yeah. I mean, I know of them. I've heard of them." He looked down at James. "Why is Talonwood working with the crows?"

"Because they're the rogues the panthers have been hunting."

"The fucking Talonwood Pack are the rogues? Are you shitting me?" Koda said, rubbing a hand down his stubble.

"How bad is this?" Daxon asked.

"Pretty fucking bad. Explains why you can't seem to end them. Their Pack is fucking huge."

"Shit," Brax said, pulling Campbell closer as if there was a threat right there in the cabin.

"How many?" Aron asked. His eyes darted to Charlie's face and then back to Koda.

"I don't know. It was in the twenties and growing when I knew them. And that was…what…fifteen or twenty years ago."

"I've never noticed any birds going nuts when I hunted. Even before I met you guys," Campbell said, turning to look at her mate then to Aron. "I would've noticed a bunch of chirping."

"I haven't, either," Daxon said.

Aron and Brax both shook their heads.

"Is this a new thing? The crows and wolves teaming up?" Gray asked.

"I didn't know they were," Koda said. His eyes moved to the window and he nodded to someone outside. "Excuse me."

Koda left the cabin, pulling the door shut behind him.

All attention turned to James.

"Do you know anything else useful?" Mason asked. It was odd to Charlie he'd been so quiet up to this point. He was usually the most talkative one of the Pride.

"If you're going to kill me, please find Beth. Get her away from those assholes," James said.

"We're not going to kill you," Charlie said.

All heads whipped around and everyone gawked at her.

"We're *not*. No one's killing him. He's a kid. He did what he had to to protect his sister. Any of you would've done the same thing for someone you love."

The males suddenly looked uncomfortable, fidgeting and coming just shy of shuffling their feet. She was right. She knew she was right. Because she would've done even worse if it had kept her family alive.

She'd only been a girl when they'd been killed. Younger than Beth. There was nothing she could do at such a young age. Especially since a Fairy's magic didn't truly mature until after twenty-one.

Charlie watched as the Ravenwood, Big River, and Blackwater discussed where to take James and how to keep everyone safe. There was no way anyone would allow James to go to either Big River or Blackwater for the same reason they didn't want to drop him off there earlier.

That left Ravenwood.

"You could leave him here. We have more numbers than you," Koda offered when he returned from whatever business had called him away.

"I can't ask you to do that. You have a lot of females here. They'd be at risk if the crows discovered you were holding James and helping us."

"Our females are as fierce as our males. One of the things I changed when I took over as Alpha; I wanted them to be able to defend themselves against any asshole who tried to claim them without consent."

The respect shining in all the males' eyes was obvious. And Charlie was sure she had the same look on her face, as well.

In the end, James did, indeed, end up going to Ravenwood territory.

It must be hard to be an Alpha, to have to make decisions that could affect every member of the Pride. Or Pack. Or whatever group. It was evident Aron didn't like the idea of possibly luring the crows and Talonwood near Charlie.

There were only the six of them. And Brax and Aron were both super protective of their mates. Didn't matter. Both females could kick butt and take names.

"Do you think they'll follow us?" Charlie asked, scooting closer to Aron until he wrapped an arm around her shoulders.

"I've been watching the rearview mirror. I haven't seen any movement in the trees and no cars are following," Mason said from the driver's seat.

"Doesn't mean they won't know where I am," James muttered.

He kept his head turned toward the window the entire ride, deep in his thoughts, probably worried about his sister.

This time, they didn't force him to ride between two of the panthers. It appeared they no longer saw him as a threat. But it wasn't lost on Charlie they made sure there was someone between him and either of the women riding in the SUV.

"You better hope they don't," Aron said, his arm tightening around Charlie.

She nudged him with her shoulder. "This isn't his fault."

"The hell it ain't," Daxon said.

"Tell me you wouldn't do whatever it took to protect your family. Or your Pride."

Charlie could only see Daxon's profile, but she didn't miss the tick in his jaw. He didn't answer her. He couldn't lie to her.

Leaning around Aron, Charlie tapped James's arm. When he turned to look at her, she smiled softly. "We'll find her. We'll get her back to you safe."

A soft growl worked up James's throat. Charlie knew that sound wasn't directed at her.

Aron, apparently, did not.

"Growl at my mate again and I'll rip your arm from your body and beat you to death with it," he said, his panther fully in his voice and glowing eyes.

"He wasn't growling at me," Charlie said, grabbing his arm tightly before he lost control.

Would he lose control of his animal with her so close? Did he not realize how dangerous that would be for her if they started fighting right there in the back seat?

No. There was no way Aron would lose himself like that. He would never endanger her life. She believed that to her core.

****

Aron fought his panther for control. Constantly, he had to remind his animal their mate was far too close to Shift. Not to mention Campbell and the rest of his Pride were within striking distance.

Charlie trusted this young dude, but Aron wasn't so sure. There was no proof a sister even existed. His mate had a good heart. She wanted to help others, she wanted to protect people.

But it could be her downfall.

He hated the thought of bringing James into their territory, but he refused to put anyone else in harm's way. This was Ravenwood's cross to bear, so to speak.

One of them needed to stand watch at all times, even in the middle of the night. They couldn't let themselves be caught off guard by the crows or by Talonwood. There were far more of them than there were of Ravenwood. It would take only minutes for the panthers and the women to be overrun and killed.

Or worse. The men would be killed and the women taken by the rogues.

That would be way worse than death.

The lights were off inside the trailer when Mason pulled onto Ravenwood territory. They didn't tend to leave lights on when they left because they usually got home around dawn. It was barely two in the morning. And Aron was wired and fully awake. There was little chance he'd get any sleep with James being so close to his mate.

"I'll take first watch," Aron announced.

Daxon waved him off. "Go be with your mate. I got first watch. And your ass is sleeping right there," he said to James, pointing to the floor by the couch.

Before anyone else could argue, Charlie brought in a blanket and pillow for James while Daxon propped himself on the couch, flipping the TV on while keeping it almost silent.

"You want me to stay up with you?" Brax asked as he yawned wide and obnoxiously loud.

"I'm good. Go to bed. Night, Charlie. Night, Camp. Fuck off the rest of you," he said, turning his back on the room and focusing the screen.

Aron knew he wasn't actually watching it. He wanted the illusion of someone being awake in case anyone decided to lurk around the property. Since it was turned all the way down, though, Daxon would hear it and give the Pride the chance to be on the offensive.

They should've left James with Morse Pack. They had greater numbers. Aron just couldn't bring himself to make James someone else's responsibility when Ravenwood were the ones who took him prisoner.

Charlie smiled at James and nodded at the makeshift bed she'd made for him on the floor. "You'll be safe here. We won't let anything happen to you." She looked around at everyone's expressions. "Okay. *I* won't let anything happen to you. Get some sleep. Then we'll try to figure out where your sister is being held."

How was his mate so damn sweet and compassionate? James was a Shifter. He'd been found with the same fuckers who'd taken her out of her yard with the intentions of selling her to the highest bidder. Yet, here she was, making sure he was comfortable both mentally and physically.

James's face softened as he nodded at her, then lowered to the floor and laid on his back, his eyes glued to the ceiling.

Aron wrapped an arm around Charlie's waist and guided her down the hall and toward the room they'd been sharing. "Do you want to take a shower before we go to bed?"

She shook her head as she pulled off her clothes. And it took every ounce of control to keep from pouncing on her and taking her hard and fast against the dresser. She was so damned beautiful. And both he and his panther were still riled up from the fight earlier.

"I'm tired. And I want to be able to hear if anyone sneaks up on us. I can't hear anything with the shower running."

"You won't be able to hear," Aron said, pulling his shirt over his head. "We'll hear it. Those fuckers will be silent. No way would you or Campbell be able to hear a thing if they figured out where we took James."

Charlie pulled a long, worn out t-shirt over her head, then worried her bottom lip. When she looked up at him, her eyes narrowed. "Do they know where you guys live?"

He didn't want to lie to her. But she looked so scared. Still, that was the best way to lose the trust of someone like Charlie. "I think the crows might. I don't know about the rogues. We tend to drive instead of Shifting and roaming the town from here, so it'd be harder to pick up our scents."

She went back to chewing on her bottom lip, and Aron wanted nothing more than to wrap her in his arms and promise her everything would be fine.

He couldn't do that, though. He had no idea if everything would be fine. He had no idea if the crows or the rogues knew where Ravenwood lived. He had no idea whether either group would come looking for James.

What was their end game with the kid? It didn't appear he had any connection. James had said he and his sister had had nowhere to go when Clint found them. He'd said it was only the two of them. And he wasn't exactly big or fast. Hell, the Pride had taken him on with ease. In fact, Aron was pretty sure Campbell had been the one to take him down, but wasn't one hundred percent positive.

"I won't let anything happen to you." That he could promise her. He'd send her away, make the Big River Pack or Blackwater Clan take her in and protect her if he had to. He'd lay his own fucking life on the line to keep her safe.

"And I won't let anything happen to you," she said.

His amazingly strong mate. Once again, he couldn't help but wonder how the hell he'd gotten so lucky as to find someone like her as a mate.

Charlie pulled the blanket back and climbed into bed. She'd made his bed every day since she'd started staying with the Pride. He'd tried to tell her she didn't need to do that, that it would get messed up again as soon as they turned in for the night. But she had said she wanted to feel like she was doing something to earn her place in the Pride's home.

He'd told her it was her home, too. But they both knew that wasn't true. She had an adorable house that was twice the size of the single wide trailer. It wasn't big at all, but that showed how small of a place the panthers were sharing. Even Brax and Campbell spent most nights at her place in House Springs.

Aron shoved his jeans down his legs and climbed into bed beside Charlie in nothing but his boxer briefs. Her eyes roamed his body until it was covered with the sheet and bedspread. She rolled onto her side and scooted until she was nuzzled under his arm and against his side.

Resting her chin on his chest, she tilted her face to look up at him. "This is going to be a long night."

"How do you figure?" he asked with a frown.

"Are you tired?"

Not really. No. He wasn't. "My body is."

"Exactly. Physically, I'm exhausted. I'm pretty sure I'd barely get a breeze if I called my magic forward right now. But my mind is wide awake and racing."

He nodded and rolled his head to look up at the dark ceiling. His mind was doing the same. And most of the thoughts revolved around how to keep his mate and Campbell safe, alive, and out of the hands of the rogues.

Amazingly, as Charlie gently scraped her nails back and forth against Aron's chest, he felt his eyes growing heavy and his body relaxed into the mattress.

Charlie was like his own brand of drug. Heady and strong and oh so good.

As sleep grew closer, he'd feared nightmares would plague him nonstop. Instead, he found peace. In fact, he couldn't remember a single dream in the few hours he slept.

He had meant to stay awake, to stay alert and listen for danger. But his panther must have realized Daxon would stay on the lookout and would keep the women and the Pride safe. Because he slept hard until Charlie nudged him awake four hours later.

"What's wrong?" he asked, moving to sit up.

Her hand pushed him back gently. "Nothing. You were pinning me to the bed, and I have to use the bathroom," she said with a soft chuckle.

While waiting for her to return, Aron stretched and rolled to a sitting position. Straining his ears, he listened for anything out of the ordinary.

He could hear Charlie in the bathroom. He could hear Mason snoring. He could hear Campbell telling Brax it was just Charlie in the bathroom – he must've woken at the sound of her moving through the trailer. No sounds of the television. No masculine conversations. No cracking of twigs or dried leaves outside. No crows squawking in the trees.

They were safe. For now.

When Charlie returned, she crawled back into bed. "Stay with me a little longer. I'm not ready to get up yet."

She sounded so sleepy. He wasn't even sure she'd opened her eyes while ambling to the bathroom and back.

Aron knew he wouldn't get any more sleep, but wasn't quite ready to leave his mate's side yet. If she wanted to stay in bed, he'd stay with her a while.

Pulling her close, he wrapped an arm around her side and nuzzled his face into her hair. He could stay like this for the rest of his life.

He just hoped they would have a lot longer than a few days left together.

Chapter Eleven

Charlie stretched her arms over her head, then smoothed them down the cool sheets beside her. She was alone.

Sitting up on her elbows, she looked to the side where Aron had slept, then looked toward the door. It was closed, and soft, masculine voices trailed through the wood.

She picked up her phone and glanced at the time, then sat straight up in the bed. They'd let her sleep until almost ten a.m. She'd only meant to doze for a few more minutes when she had come back to bed. What the heck? Why didn't they wake her up?

Throwing the blankets off, she sat up and grabbed a clean set of clothes from her suitcase, then hurried to the bathroom for a quick shower. She was hungry and wanted to know if they'd heard anything while she had slept.

Charlie washed her hair and body as fast as she could, forgoing the razor that sat on the side of the tub, then dried off just as quickly. She wanted to get some information and make sure Aron was out there waiting for her and hadn't run off on his own.

Surely, he would've woken her if he was going to take James somewhere or was going to watch the perimeter of Ravenwood territory while everyone else slept.

Donning a pair of clean jeans, a sweatshirt, and roughly combed hair, Charlie pulled the door open and almost jogged into the living room...

To find the entire group at the table with coffee mugs and empty plates sitting in front of them.

"You didn't wake me for breakfast?" she asked, searching the table for bowls or skillets with leftover food.

"I made you a plate," Aron said, standing and pulling a heaping plate from the microwave. "It's still warm."

He set the plate at the spot beside him, then waited for her to sit before he took his own chair.

"What's going on?" she asked before shoveling a forkful of scrambled eggs in her mouth.

"We're getting company today," Daxon answered.

Charlie stiffened with another forkful of food halfway to her mouth. "They found us?"

Aron shook his head and laid his arm across the back of her chair. "Koda is sending a bunch of his best fighters to hang out with us for a while until we can figure out what to do with him." He nodded toward James, who sat on the floor, his back to the wall, staring through the front window.

"Didn't you offer him some food?"

"Yeah. He didn't want it."

Well, that wouldn't do. "James, come join us. There's plenty on my plate. I'll share with you."

"Thank you. But I'm not hungry." His voice sounded as sad as his eyes looked. He was worried about his sister. Worried about the threat to her since he was no longer doing the bidding of the crows and the Talonwood.

Her heart broke for him. She knew the feeling of utter helplessness. She knew the feeling of loss.

"You sure? There's plenty left."

Aron frowned at her from his chair. She knew he didn't want her to give up her food for a possible enemy, but she couldn't stand the thought of the young man going hungry.

James shook his head and gave her a sad smile, then went back to staring through the front window.

With a heavy sigh, Charlie went back to eating. She lacked the gusto she'd had when she first sat down. "We have to find his sister."

"She's with the rest of the assholes. There aren't nearly enough of us to crash their camp to rescue her. And that's if we could even find where they're hiding out," Daxon said, rubbing the back of his neck.

Everyone looked tense. Except Mason. He was the picture of relaxed as he leaned back in his chair, his hands folded over his stomach, an amused smile on his lips.

"It would be fun, though," he said, his smile growing.

"What would be?" Campbell asked.

"Invading their camp and taking all those fuckers out."

"And what if there are more like James?" Charlie asked. She refused to punish those who were innocent. Even if they had been a part of taking women against their will.

"There are," James said softly from his spot against the wall.

All eyes turned to him. He didn't say anything else.

"Fuck," Brax whispered as he pushed his wayward hair from his face. "How many others are being blackmailed into helping them?" he asked James.

James finally turned to look at the group at the table. "At least six more. The crows, that guy Clint, they're real good at making people feel safe. They offer shelter and protection. Then they use your sister, your daughter, whoever, to force you into doing whatever the fuck he wants. Even if that means putting other females through what your family is currently going through." Tears welled in his eyes as he spoke. He quickly turned his head away so no one would see his weakness.

"Do you know how many members there are?" Daxon asked.

It took James a few minutes to answer. When he looked back, his lashes were damp, his eyes were red, but no tears stained his cheeks.

"Of which group?"

"Either. Both," Daxon said, leaning forward and resting his forearms on the table.

James's eyes lowered as he seemed to count in his head. "The crows have at least twenty. The Talonwood Pack have dwindled to around thirteen. That's why they keep grabbing people like me and Beth. There aren't many people who want to be a part of their fucked up plans."

The F word sounded strange coming from his young, innocent face.

"So somewhere around thirty or so," Campbell said.

James nodded.

"How many can we get?" Campbell asked Aron.

"What?"

"We have a lot of friends. How many do you think would help us?"

"We can't ask everyone to risk their lives to help us," Aron said.

"Why not? We've always helped them every chance we could. Shit. Daxon and I came back from KC to help when that Fairy bitch tried to run off with Hollyn," Brax said.

Aron pulled the arm from the back of Charlie's chair and scratched the stubble that peppered his cheeks and jaw. He looked deep in thought. He also looked tormented with the decision he had to make.

"We can't ask Gray, Reed, or Colton," he said, although it looked like he was talking to himself more than the Pride.

"That's fair enough. Hell, Tristan's mate Peyton might be enough to end it within minutes," Campbell teased.

"Is her wolf really that crazy?" Charlie asked, her gaze bouncing from person to person.

All eyes were wide as they all nodded. Mason shivered jokingly. "I wouldn't want to fight her."

"You wouldn't fight her, anyway," Campbell said with a roll of her eyes.

"Five of us–"

"Six," Charlie corrected.

Aron looked at her and she could see the fear for his mate blazing bright in his glowing green eyes. "Six of us. We'll see how many Koda can spare. Noah. Luke. Carter. Maybe Tristan and Peyton."

"What about Eli and Emory?" Brax asked.

"Emory's pretty small," Daxon said.

"Yeah, but she's a bad ass," Campbell said with a smile. "Don't discount us women. We can kick ass, too."

Campbell reached across the table for a high five from Charlie. Charlie slapped her hand with a wide grin.

"Yeah!" And then she had a thought. "Hollyn and I can team up and cause a lot of mayhem. We have magic you guys don't."

"I doubt Noah will want his mate in the middle of a fight," Mason said.

"It's not Noah's choice. You all fought for females to have a choice in their life. She can make the decision on whether she wants to be a part of this or not," Campbell said, jutting her chin out indignantly.

Mason had a crooked grin as he held his hands up in surrender. "I didn't say *I* didn't want her to fight. I said Noah is protective of his mate."

"So are Brax and Aron," Charlie pointed out. "And every single mated male."

"We can ask them for backup while we get the women out and try to liberate the men they're blackmailing. They don't have to go in with us, just be there in case things go sideways," Campbell said.

James had turned now and was watching them intently. "You're really going to get Beth out? I'll do anything you want. I swear on my own life. I'll be your fucking slave for years; I'll do your laundry and be your personal chef for the rest of my life if you get her to safety."

"Where will you guys go once we get her out?" Charlie asked. She refused to say *if*. The only option was to get the young girl out, along with the rest of the women. Anything else would be a complete and total failure and something Charlie refused to accept.

He shrugged. "I don't know, but Beth staying alive is more important."

Charlie noticed he hadn't mentioned his own fate hanging in the balance, but decided not to comment because, if she had her way, both he and his sister would be safe.

****

Aron and Daxon made some phone calls and sent out texts. Gray wanted to help, but Aron refused to allow it. He needed to stay with his mate and cub. So did Reed. And Colton needed to stay with his very pregnant and fragile mate.

They decided to send Colton and Shawnee to Big River territory. Talonwood had never been there and it might be safter for the cubs and Shawnee.

Koda showed up within minutes of Aron talking to Gray and brought fifteen males and three females. That was eighteen more to help them in what seemed like an impossible task.

That now put their numbers at thirty-four with the bears, wolves, and all their mates. Way, *way* better than the original six of Ravenwood. They might have a chance now.

"You sure about them?" Brax said, nodding toward the three females lingering nearby.

"We can hear you," one of the women said.

Mason grinned wide. "I like her," he said.

The woman rolled her eyes and looked away from Mason.

"They're fierce. They've fought their share of battles. And they want to help get those women out of the clutches of the rogues," Koda said.

"Is there really a sixteen-year-old being held?" one of the females asked.

"And a fourteen-year-old," James supplied. "They're using her to make her father help Talonwood and Black Feather."

"Fuck," Koda said, running a hand down his growing beard.

Introductions were made. Hands were shaken. Welcomes and thanks were issued.

"When do we do this?" Koda asked.

"Tonight. When the sun sets so there's less possibility of any humans spotting us," Aron answered.

The mated pairs went off on their own while everyone else went over plans and logistics.

Aron took Charlie's hand and led her into the woods, far enough away they could no longer hear the conversations and no one could hear them.

"What's wrong?" Charlie asked when they were far enough away. She didn't need to be an empath to feel the fear and anxiety rolling from Aron in waves.

"Is there any way I can convince you to stay back in Big River?" he asked as they slowed to a stroll, their hands entwined as they moved through the woods.

"What? No. Why would I stay back while you guys fight?"

"If I said I wanted you to stay back to help keep the babies safe would you believe me?" he asked, turning his head slightly to look down at her.

Her brows dropped and she pulled her hand from his. Stopping, she crossed her arms over her chest and glared at him.

"Take that as a no." He ran his hand down his face.

"I know you're worried about me. But guess what? I'm worried about you, too. You said it would destroy you if something happened to me. Do you really think I could go about my life as if everything was great if I lost you? Really? I thought I made it perfectly clear how much I love you."

He reached for her, but she pulled away.

"I need you to say you understand. I need to know you support me in doing this."

This time, when Aron reached for her, she didn't pull away. Wrapping his arms around her back, he pulled her close. "I support you in everything, Charlie. That doesn't mean I like it or want you in the thick of shit. But I'll never demand you change."

Charlie rested her head against his chest and listened to his heart beat. The thought of that heart stopping brought tears to her eyes.

She had to trust in her friends. She had to trust they'd all watch each other's backs.

Maybe they'd get lucky. Maybe they'd be able to sneak in, help the women escape, then sneak out before anyone discovered they were there. And then the men who were being held against their will could flip the rogues the middle finger and be on their way. There would be nothing holding them there anymore.

****

Aron had never felt as much fear before as he did right now. It was bad enough when Charlie had gone hunting with them for the first time. Now, they were talking about going after the entire group of rogues. And it wasn't only one Pack. The crows were involved.

They had no idea whether Black Feather Crew stayed with Talonwood or not. But he'd bet his left fucking nut that had been them in the woods last night when they'd found Talonwood trying to take off with Teresa. They'd gotten real fucking loud when James had started talking.

The crows in their Shifted form would be no match against big fucking cats. Or wolves. Or bears. So, would they stay in their human forms? Or would they be cowards and dive bomb everyone, going for their eyes and faces?

He already knew they were cowards. No real man would ever imprison a woman. No real man would sell a woman or mistreat her in any way.

Women were queens and should be treated as such.

Aron racked his brain, trying to think of anything and everything that he could use to convince Charlie to stay back.

In the end, though, he knew there was no way she would avoid this fight. It was personal to her. She didn't have to say that for him to know she was trying to help the women who were taken the same way she was.

The huge difference was she was saved before they'd gotten her away. She had been saved the same fate of so many others, like Campbell's sister who had been killed during a forced Shift.

What horrors had those women gone through, the ones being used to blackmail their brothers and fathers? Had the rogues hurt them? Beat them?

Raped them?

Anger built on top of the fear until his face hurt and his veins burned with adrenaline and rage. His gums throbbed with the fangs that wanted to drop into his mouth. His panther snarled, growled, hissed in his head. Both sides of him were ready to end this shit.

But would it ever end? Would females, both human and otherwise, ever be safe? Would they ever be able to walk alone at night without worrying some psycho was waiting to pull them into a dark alley?

He knew the answer to that. No. They wouldn't.

Guess it was a good thing his mate had her magic. And he respected the fact Koda let females from his Pack fight. They would be less likely to become victims since they knew how to protect themselves.

Charlie could protect herself, yet she'd still been caught off guard.

That anger and fear multiplied.

Until Charlie tightened her hold. Her arms were wrapped around his back, her cheek pressed firmly against his chest.

Aron rested his left cheek on top of her head and inhaled her scent. He wanted to stay like this, just him and Charlie, her small body pressed against his, her arms holding him.

"We should get back," Charlie said, snapping him out of his thoughts.

"I was literally just thinking I wanted to stay like this," Aron said, pulling back to look down at her.

Charlie's lashes were wet and her eyes were welled with tears.

"What's wrong?"

"I already told you – I'm worried about you. I don't want to lose you." Her voice hitched on a sob and she moved back in to press her face against his chest.

The depth of her sorrow hit Aron right in the fucking heart. She'd told him she was worried about him but didn't realize how deep that ran.

"Fuck," he muttered under his breath.

Charlie pulled back and frowned up at him.

"We're a mess. We can't be distracted tonight, honey. You got to keep your focus on what's going on around you. Don't worry about me. I'll be fine. I've done this for a long time."

"Right back at you," she said with a soft smile. "Don't let my presence distract you. Hollyn and I are a force to be reckoned with."

Aron reached up and wiped a tear from her cheek that had rolled over her lashes.

All that mattered was Charlie surviving the night. He knew his Pride and the rest of his friends would keep an eye on her. But he didn't want to lose any of them. Not a single one.

If only there was a way to do this without dragging everyone else into the fucking fire with him.

Chapter Twelve

Charlie watched the Alphas speak in low tones near the trucks. They were trying to decide how close to get in their vehicles and where the safest spot would be to Shift. Campbell, Charlie, and Hollyn would follow, bringing up the rear.

As scared as she was of what was about to happen, a strange, excited buzz moved through her limbs. It was as though her magic knew exactly what was coming and was ready to be called forth to cause some damage to Talonwood. The crows, too.

They had all argued over whether to refrain from killing anyone. There were too many chances of taking out someone who was there against their will, too many who were there to protect someone they loved.

In the end, though, they decided their main goal was to save as many women as possible. Charlie and Campbell agreed they shouldn't leave until they found every single female there.

The thought of killing an innocent person made her sick, but if they fought alongside the others, there would be no way to tell.

Would they fight? If they realized everyone was there to liberate the women, would they stand beside the rogues and fight or would they switch sides?

She couldn't think of a single reason they would continue to fight on the side of the same creeps who had imprisoned the women they loved. No way.

"You sure about this?" Aron asked as he neared her.

Campbell rolled her eyes and moved to stand with Brax. Charlie wasn't the only one with estrogen. Counting herself, there were nine women.

Charlie wouldn't admit this aloud for fear of offending Peyton, but she couldn't wait to see Cujo in action. If Peyton's wolf was as volatile as everyone said, they might only need *her* to win the fight.

Feeling a little ashamed for even thinking about wanting to see the sweet blonde in battle, Charlie followed the group to the various trucks and cars. They loaded as many as possible in each to avoid a long line of vehicles and making themselves too obvious.

Even with the large amount of carpooling, they still ended up taking more than what would remain inconspicuous.

"We're going to park about two miles down the road," Aron explained to Mason, who once again drove the SUV the Pride was squeezed into, along with two females from Morse Pack.

Mason nodded. His usual light demeanor was gone. The fun-loving Pride member was nowhere to found. Now, in the driver's seat, a serious and ready for battle Shifter clutched the steering wheel until his knuckles were white.

Aron's arm was tight around Charlie's shoulders. She kept seeing him watch her from her periphery. She was doing her best to ignore the risks and focus on the job the Alphas had given her – watch the front line's backs, keep an eye on the rear, and make sure no one was overrun or outnumbered.

Seemed easy enough. But the memories of last night, of seeing so many wolves on the backs of the people she'd grown to love made her stomach turn until she was worried she would have to roll down a window or ask Mason to pull over so she could puke.

She tried to think of the numbers behind her. There were six from Ravenwood Pride. The eighteen wolf Shifters from Morse Pack. Carter and June, Luke and Piper, and Noah and Hollyn from Blackwater Clan. Tristan and Peyton and Micah and Callie from Big River. Then there was Emory and Eli from Hope Pride.

All in all, they'd brought along a bunch of predator Shifters and angry men and women who were ready to stand against the evil and chaos that followed Talonwood and Black Feather. Wolf and crow Shifters.

Total cowards.

That helped her nerves. In their place was rage. A rage so hot it burned through her veins until she wondered if she hadn't inherited some of Hollyn's fire. As much as she loved her wind, she had been mildly jealous as a child. She had wished she could blow flames like a dragon. She'd wished she could've charred the people who had taken her entire family from her.

"Are we even sure the rogues are there?" Mason asked as he led the line of cars.

Charlie was snapped out of her thoughts.

"What?" Aron asked.

"What information are we going on? James's testimony? You sure he's not leading us into some bull shit?"

James was currently riding with the bears. Even in their human form, Noah, Luke, and Carter were massive and intimidating.

"Why would he lie? His little sister is being held there," Charlie said, leaning forward between the front seats.

"He *said* his sister is being held there. This could be total crap," Mason said.

He glanced over his shoulder before turning his focus back to the dark road. It was windy with a lot of hills. One missed curve and they'd careen into the ditch or smash into an oncoming car. Not that there were a whole lot of cars out this late.

"I'll check it out before we all go crashing in to their camp," Aron said.

Charlie's head whipped around. "You're not going in there alone, Aron."

He kept saying how worried he was about her then was going to volunteer to serve himself up on a silver platter to the same people who'd taken her with the intent on selling her into slavery?

Not a chance.

"I'll go with him," Daxon said.

"Me, too," Brax said.

"Doesn't make me feel better," Charlie said, crossing her arms over her chest and dropping back against the seat. "I should go with you. At least then I can use my magic to keep the jerks away if they catch you snooping."

"Nope," Aron said.

"You're not even my mate and that shit is getting on my nerves," Campbell said. "How is it you guys think you're all these major badasses, you say women are queens, then you treat us like we're made of porcelain or something. I've seen with my own eyes what she's capable of, and so have you. I say we go as a Pride and let the rest hang back for more information."

Charlie turned and smiled at Campbell. She smiled back and nodded.

"Sisters got to stick together," she said with a shrug.

Sisters. She'd never had a sister. She'd had a brother. She'd had girl cousins. But now, she finally had a real sister, even if it wasn't by blood.

"Fuck," Brax muttered from beside his mate.

"You serious?" Daxon asked, turning all the way in his seat to glare at Campbell. "It's bad enough these two will be watching you guys the whole time. Now –"

"We can watch our dang selves," Charlie said. "And *we* can watch over *you*."

She knew it wasn't the best argument, but it was all she could come up with on the spot. She was getting tired of these guys acting as if the women would get in the way or something.

Okay. So they didn't quite act like they'd get in the way, but they did call them distractions. Did they not realize it was just as hard to fight without worrying about their guys?

Charlie loved Aron. She'd lay her life down for him. But she would do the same for her new Pride, as well. It was as scary for her to know they would be in harm's way as it was for them to think of the women in harm's way.

Huh. Maybe that was what she should've said instead.

Mason pulled the SUV into a dark, empty parking lot. All the trucks and cars followed.

Koda, Carter, Aron, and Micah met in front of the Pride's SUV, their faces and bodies lit by the headlights.

Charlie rolled her window down and listened as Aron quietly told them the new plan.

"We need to make sure we're close enough in case there's trouble," Micah said, his eyes even brighter than normal. He always looked so intense and a tad scary. Charlie couldn't help but be thankful he was on their side.

Aron's eyes darted to Charlie's in the back seat. "My Pride will get as close as we can to make sure James wasn't full of shit. If it's clear, I'll Shift. The second you get wind of my fur, move in. We'll go as quickly and quietly as possible. First priority is getting the females out. Only attack if attacked."

"What about the others, man?" Koda asked. "I don't feel right about killing someone if they don't want to be a part of this shit."

Aron dragged a hand down his face and glanced back at Charlie again. "If they attack you, defend yourself. Any innocent man won't truly fight. Even if they're trying to make it look like they're going along with whatever game Talonwood and Black Feather are playing... We've fought others who had no choice. They never struck a killing blow. But don't let anyone take you down, either. And keep your eyes on the trees. They could have a crow or two watching out for trouble. If they alert the fuckers, we'll have no choice but to go to war."

The other Alphas nodded. Manly handshakes were exchanged. Then Aron came back to the SUV and climbed in beside Charlie.

"You guys sure you all want to go?"

"Absolutely," Charlie said.

The rest of the Pride nodded. There was no way anyone in the Pride would let the Alpha put himself in danger without being there to back him up. Shoot. She didn't think they'd let *any* member of the Pride go in alone. That was how they were. All of them. Every single Shifter she'd gotten to know were loyal. And not only to their own families.

Mason crept the vehicle forward another mile or so, then pulled off onto what looked like an abandoned road. He drove until there were more trees than road, then pulled between two large oaks to give the rest of the Shifters room to park.

Doors were softly shut. It was almost creepy how quietly they all moved, even with the dead leaves littering the forest floor.

No one said a word. Aron motioned to the Alphas, pointed at each member of the Pride, then held his hand out to Charlie, palm out, making sure she knew not to follow to closely.

The panthers pulled their clothes off and dropped them onto the hood of the truck in case he needed to Shift. Charlie would have loved to ogle her mate in all his naked glory, but her mind was too focused on the fear of losing him tonight.

Don't think like that. Keep that out of your head.

She didn't have the talent of manifestation. So her thoughts wouldn't turn into reality. Still. She didn't want to put any bad energy into the universe and cause anyone to get hurt or killed.

Both Aron and Brax glanced at their mates before padding silently further into the woods.

Campbell and Charlie nodded at each other, giving the other a visual pep talk, then followed the men at a distance. The women had to be far more careful of where their feet landed to avoid the rogues and crows from hearing their approach.

By the time Charlie caught up to Aron and the rest of the guys, they were crouched on their knees watching several single wide trailers. There were lights on in a few of them. People milled around. But she couldn't tell whether these were the rogues or simply another group of Shifters.

As far as she knew, it could be a group of humans. She didn't have the sense of smell the Shifters had.

Campbell put out her arm, telling Charlie to stop. They were about twenty yards from where Aron and the rest of the guys were, but they were stealthy. The smallest crack of a twig could alert the enemy of their approach.

Aron looked over at Daxon.

Slinking backward, the men kept their eyes on the camp as they neared the women. Campbell took Charlie's arm and pulled her backward. They tiptoed ahead of the guys, making sure no one was sneaking up behind them while Aron and the others watched their backs.

Like they'd explained in the SUV – the women could watch over the guys as much as they looked over the women. It was team work in the truest sense.

****

Aron still hated the thought of Charlie out here with only the five other Pride members as back up against the entirety of the Talonwood rogues and their asshole buddies, Black Feather.

But as the Pride inched away from their camp, it was reassuring to know Charlie and Campbell were back there making sure no one was hiding in wait to take them out before they could Shift and let everyone else know the situation.

The second they were all far enough to keep from being detected, Aron turned and joined his mate, walking so close his side brushed against her hip. Her fingers twined through his and he could feel the tension rolling from her. But it was more than fear…he could feel her excitement.

His mate was excited to liberate the women imprisoned by the rogues. That both terrified him and made him so fucking proud to have Charlie in his life. She was so strong, even after being a victim herself.

She wasn't a victim. She never was. She was a survivor. A fucking fighter.

And now, she wanted to give these other women a chance to fight for their life.

Aron could smell fur as he neared his friends. Someone had Shifted. When he met up with the group, he realized the bears had already Shifted and waited to run into battle to protect the Pride.

Good friends. Loyal friends.

"They're there. I couldn't tell whether Black Feather is staying there, but Talonwood has definitely set up camp right under our fucking noses."

"How the fuck did they pull that off?" Koda asked, his eyes bright as his wolf tried to push through. "How did we not know they were so damn close?"

Whether he was speaking to himself or asking one of them a question, Aron didn't know. And he didn't have the answer. He was pissed at his own self for not knowing how many women were being held in his own back yard.

It wasn't literally his back yard. But it was close enough he should have known. He should have stopped the rogues. He should have protected all those women.

"It's not your fault," Charlie muttered, looking up into Aron's face. It was as though his mate could read his thoughts. "None of this is your fault. There is no way any of you could have had any idea what these guys were doing."

Aron looked around. Those who were still in human form looked as if they felt the same way he did – ashamed. Ashamed that the rogues were so close and they hadn't been able to stop them.

They couldn't dwell on that now. They had a job to do. And there was no way he would leave without every single one of those women being held prisoner to those sick, twisted assholes.

"There are at least twelve women. They were all being held in the same trailer. Every single place is a single wide mobile home, and it seems a few are empty," Aron said.

"Waiting for more slaves?" Peyton said.

Aron glanced at her, then did a double take. "Will you be able to control your wolf until it's necessary?"

She nodded, but it was a jerky movement. It was the best he could ask for at the moment. His own panther was clawing at his insides to be released so he could go back into Talonwood territory.

"What about the crows?"

"I didn't see any of Black Feather. And I didn't see any of them in the trees. They might not be living here."

"Distancing themselves?" one of Koda's men said as he tilted his head side to side with audible pops.

"Plausible deniability," Koda muttered. He rubbed the back of his neck and rolled his neck in a similar fashion as his Pack brother.

"I don't know. But that gives us better odds," Aron said.

He looked around, then down at his mate. He was tempted to ask again if she'd stay back. But that would leave her alone. It would be too easy for someone to veer off, scent her on the wind, and disappear with her before he even knew she was gone.

No way would these assholes stop unless they were stopped.

And Aron would do everything in his power to make sure it was over tonight.

"Get all the women out. If we're detected, take out anyone who gets in your way." Charlie nudged his side. With a sigh, Aron said, "Try not to kill any male who isn't either fighting in earnest or fighting at all."

"What do we do with those who surrender?" Eli asked.

Shit. He hadn't thought about that. He hadn't even considered it a possibility. Low life assholes like the rogues didn't just give themselves up and beg for mercy. They were in it for money and power.

"I guess take them for now. We're sort it out later," Aron said.

"We'll take them to Morse Pack territory. We have greater numbers and there are no pups in our Pack."

Aron dipped his head once in acknowledgement and appreciation. He'd heard about what Koda had done when Reed's mate had been harassed by a male attempting to force her into a pairing. He was a good Alpha.

"Same deal. We'll go ahead. Charlie, Campbell, and Hollyn take the rear, but stay close in case anyone tries to sneak up on us. Hollyn, watch your flames. I don't want my fur singed. Keep yourselves safe, but don't let anyone get overrun." He hadn't released his hold on Charlie the entire time he spoke with the group. Even now, when it was time to move forward, he found himself reluctant to release her.

Could he maintain his focus with his mate so close to so many psychos? He had to. That was the only way he could truly protect her was by keeping his head in the game and making sure he made it home with her tonight.

As long as *she* made it home tonight. He knew his Pride would take care of her until she was ready to move on.

Fuck. Even the thought of her with another man after his death was like a punch to his nuts.

Pops and cracks filled the silence as each human Shifted into his or her animal. Aron bent and pressed a hard kiss to Charlie's lips.

"Be safe," he pushed out as his animal began to take over. "I love you."

Those were the last words he could get out before his mouth filled with fangs, fur sprouted from his body, and his bones broke and reshaped until he was standing on four legs instead of two.

Aron slank his body along Charlie's, a silent expression of his affection, then trotted to catch up with his friends who'd already began to creep forward.

With one glance back, he ensured the human and two Fae were following directions and staying far enough back yet close enough for someone to help if there was some kind of sneak attack.

That was all he'd allow himself for now. He had to trust she was smart and strong. She and the others could take care of themselves. Hell. Campbell had been kicking ass long before she'd ever met the panthers. And Hollyn and Charlie could turn someone into a fire tornado.

Eyes forward, he mentally prepared for what was to come. And prayed they'd all make it out alive.

Chapter Thirteen

Charlie's hands trembled as she followed the large group of animals. Her eyes scanned over the many species. There were the panthers, wolves, bears, a female lion, a leopard, and a large male lion complete with an impressive rusty orange mane. If any humans were to wander upon them, they'd think there was some kind of zoo escape.

The display of dominant power was impressive. She might not have been a Shifter, but she could feel the dominance rolling from every single person there. For a brief second, she felt sorry for the rogues if this turned into a fight.

That feeling was fleeting.

No way could she feel sorry for assholes who would take women for their own monetary gain or to turn them into their own personal baby makers.

Hollyn was on Charlie's right, Campbell on her left. The female Shifters were toward the back...except for Peyton's wolf. The animal just about attacked anyone who tried to coax her toward the back.

As much as Charlie wanted to declare chauvinism about the women being in the back line, she kind of liked the huge force of females. It was their job to make sure the men weren't outnumbered. And it would be their job to get the women to the vehicles, even if the fight was still ongoing.

All she could do as they neared the territory was pray the men who were being coerced into working with the Talonwood wouldn't fight.

But what if they thought it was simply another group trying to capitalize on the rogues endeavors? What if they thought Charlie and her friends were there to take the women and make money from them?

James. James was slinking between two of the bears in his wolf form. They would see he was with them. They would have to know he would never hurt his own sister.

And Charlie didn't doubt for one second he was telling the truth about a younger sister being taken and held.

All movement ceased. Charlie, Hollyn, and Campbell stopped about twenty feet back and waited. They didn't have the hearing the Shifters did. Raising her eyes, Charlie searched the trees for those crows who'd been watching them when they'd found Teresa and taken James for questioning.

The woods were silent. Even the nocturnal bugs and animals were silent as if they knew something big was coming.

Silver light shone through the bare trees from the full moon overhead. That was the only light she and the other two women had to help them navigate through the thick and dark woods. And the only thing that kept them from tripping over a fallen log and letting the enemy know someone was in there.

Shoot. She should've suggested using one of the women as bait to get some of Talonwood out in the woods and away from their friends. She knew Aron, Brax, and Noah would have fought against it, but it would've helped.

Too late now.

Charlie strained to hear anything that would have made the Shifters stop. She squinted her eyes, looking toward the front, looking for Aron. All she could see was a sea of dark fur with a dot of golden fur from Eli's giant lion.

Glancing to each side of her, she realized Hollyn and Campbell were doing the same thing. They must have been as nervous as she was about their mates being up front while all they could do was wait to see if they were needed.

This whole thing was nerve wracking.

Yet, that same excited energy buzzed through Charlie's veins.

She knew she wasn't excited to fight. And she sure wasn't excited to see her mate or friends fight. She was merely excited to liberate all those women being held inside Talonwood territory.

Leaves crunched softly to her left. All heads whipped to that side. A few growls sounded somewhere in front of her, then blurs whipped around her. As hard as she tried, she couldn't figure out who was where and what the hell was going on.

Then a loud cacophony of squawks sounded from overhead. The crows were there. They'd been hidden somewhere among the trees and watched her friends' approach.

Oh no.

Had they walked into a trap?

Running to catch up to where her friends were now fighting, she frantically scanned the writhing bodies until she found Aron. He was okay. He was fighting one on one with a wolf and it looked like he was winning.

Hollyn darted to the left. Charlie followed her with her eyes, making sure no one tried to grab her or jump on her.

A large bear was fighting a large wolf while two clung to his back. It must have been Noah for Hollyn to panic the way she had.

Holding her hands out, Charlie waited to see if Hollyn needed her wind. She should've known better. Her cousin had total control of her fire and was able to burn only those who were piled on top of her mate without Noah getting so much as a singed hair.

Campbell darted forward, a gun held in her right hand. She aimed it and...*boom*!

A few Shifters winced and ducked, while the rest continued their battle. They weren't going to let anyone abscond with their money makers.

Charlie wasn't sure who Campbell shot or if she even hit anyone. Maybe she was trying to scare them. Either way, the fighting continued.

Fear inched its way into her heart as crows began to dive from the trees, clawing and pecking at the faces of her friends. They weren't the size of normal crows, either. They were huge, more the size of hawks.

Okay. She had this. Raising her hands, she blew wind toward them and created a type of barrier over the war raging on the forest floor.

A few crows slammed into trees and lie limp on the ground. A few others were blown further into the woods until Charlie could no longer see then. The rest tested the strange current and then gave up, flying toward where the women were.

No way. She would not let them take those women when the Pride was so close to freeing them.

"The crows!" she screamed as she ran toward Talonwood territory.

A loud screech followed her. She knew it was Aron telling her to wait, telling her not to go alone.

But the sound of large paws slamming into the ground behind her let her know at least one bear was following close behind. She wasn't alone.

Glancing over her shoulder, she spotted a wolf running full force in her direction and prayed it was one of their friends and not a rogue. She might know Aron and the rest of the panthers in their animal forms, but she didn't know everyone else well enough to know all their markings and nuances.

As the wolf whipped past her, he glanced at her and she realized she recognized the eyes – Micah. His eyes were a different color blue than the rest of the wolves and his body was lither than the rest. What kind of wolf was he?

The lioness followed closely – Callie. She was sticking with her mate and staying close to Charlie to make sure she wasn't hurt while getting the women out.

There were only a few wolves left in the territory to guard the women while the rest fought. Raising her hands, she blew them over a hundred yards away.

The trailer they stood in front of must have been where the women were being kept. Why else would they guard it?

Charlie ran as fast as her legs would carry her, scanning the rest of the area to make sure there was no one else waiting to attack when she wasn't looking. As far as she could tell, it was now only her and the three Shifters at her back.

There were only three stairs leading up to the door to the trailer. Hand on the knob, a sense of foreboding hit her, but she pushed on and yanked it open, determined to get the women to safety so she could rejoin the fight. That had been their objective the whole time. She had the opportunity and couldn't fail.

A boom sounded and Charlie had a momentary thought that Campbell had shot another Shifter.

Screams erupted from inside the trailer. And then pain bloomed from her side and radiated to every limb.

Looking down, Charlie was confused at the dark red spreading on her shirt. She didn't remember getting near anyone who'd been hurt or bleeding.

Pain. Lots of pain. Blood.

A young woman stood across the room, her eyes wide, a gun clutched in her hands.

"Oh my God! I'm so sorry! I thought…"

Arms wrapped around Charlie and pulled her to a solid body.

Noah. Noah was in his human form and cradled her against his chest.

"I can walk," she muttered.

"You've been shot."

"Who shot me?"

She was so confused. The woman with the gun? Had she shot Charlie? Why would she do that?

I'm so sorry. I thought…

She thought what? Did she think they were there to hurt her? And where the hell did she get the gun? If she'd had it all along, why hadn't she used it to get out of there? Even with six bullets or however many that gun held, she should've been able to escape.

Not true. If these women were all human, or even mostly human, they wouldn't have been able to outrun the Shifters once they were free.

Her thoughts circled around all the facts and assumptions. And then they got foggy.

A howl pierced the night and rattled Charlie's brain. Clapping her hands over her ears, she looked around. Where was Noah taking her? He couldn't very well carry her back to the battle raging in the middle of the woods.

But she didn't hear snarls and growls. She didn't hear anything. She was conscious and from the way that howl had hurt her head she knew she hadn't gone deaf.

There had always been this weird myth in the human world that the only way to kill a Fairy was with iron.

Total myth.

While they had magic, they still bled like a human. A simple bullet or knife wound could kill Charlie as easily as it could kill Campbell.

Was she dying? She didn't feel like she was dying. She also had no idea what dying felt like.

She was definitely getting weaker. And cold. But it was the middle of November. The night was quite chilly and she'd only worn a light jacket so it wouldn't hinder her if and when she needed to use her magic.

Now she could no longer feel her magic. She couldn't even conjure a breeze. It was like when the rogues had found her and hit her hard enough to daze her.

"What the fuck happened?" someone yelled.

Charlie blinked. Her eyes were out of focus. She was falling asleep. No. She was losing consciousness. She'd promised Aron she would be careful and would stay close to the group.

She'd run off on her own to rescue the women.

Surely, he wouldn't be mad at her for that. Besides, she'd had Noah, Micah, and Callie there with her. How was she supposed to know one of the women would think she was the enemy and shoot her?

"Aron!" Campbell yelled.

Where was Aron? She was having a hard time focusing on anyone's faces or animals. They were a blur of fur and flesh as Noah carried her closer.

"Is it over?" Charlie asked as Noah adjusted her weight in his arms.

"It's over," Campbell said. "Where the fuck is Aron?"

"He's chasing down one of those bastards who ran," someone said.

Who? She didn't recognize the voice. She didn't really know Koda's men. It must have been one of them.

"Who ran? Are the good guys okay?" she asked. Her words sounded slurred in her own head.

"The good guys?" Noah grumbled, looking down into her face.

"Yeah. The guys…" She inhaled deep. Why was it getting hard to breathe? She was shot in the side, not the lungs. "The ones who didn't want to be here."

"They're fine. They didn't fight," Noah said in his gruff voice.

"You're nice," she said.

Noah's lips twitched as he frowned down at her. "Keep your eyes open, Charlie. Aron's coming."

"Where is Aron?" She was so tired. A nap. She just wanted a little nap. It had been a long day and a longer night.

"He's coming," Campbell said as she pushed Charlie's hair from her face.

"Charlie?" Hollyn said, panic in her voice. "Oh my God! What happened? Did she get bit?"

"One of the women shot her," Noah said.

"What? Why?"

"I thought...I thought you guys were coming to hurt us," a woman said.

Charlie lifted her head to look over Noah's shoulder. "We're hear to help you. You're free. Is there...is there a Beth here?"

"I'm Beth," a petite teenager said as she stepped forward.

"James is here. He brought us to help you."

Dropping her head back against Noah's chest, Charlie closed her eyes and tried to sleep. She just needed sleep.

"Open your eyes, Charlie. Look at me," Noah said, his voice humming through his chest.

She forced her lids open but was having a hard time focusing on anything or even keeping her eyes open.

"We've got to get her some help. Can Fae go to the hospital?" Campbell asked.

"Yeah," Hollyn said, taking Charlie's hand in hers. "Yeah. We have the same genetics as humans. We just happen to carry magic inside of us."

"She needs blood. And probably surgery," Noah said.

Charlie rocked and swayed. Opening her eyes, she watched the trees overhead pass her and thought the moon looked incredibly beautiful tonight. "So many stars," she whispered.

"Aron!" Campbell yelled.

"Get your ass over here!" Brax yelled louder than Campbell.

Feet thundered against the ground. Pops and cracks sounded. Then Aron's face hovered over hers. "What the fuck happened to her?" he asked, his voice full of anguish. "Were you bitten, baby? Scratched?"

"Shot. She shot me," Charlie forced past her lips.

She closed her eyes again and felt her body growing heavier.

"Don't look at me like that. It wasn't me. One of the women thought we were here to take them away and sell them. I was with you guys the whole time." That was Campbell. Charlie knew Campbell's voice. But why did it sound so far away?

"Give her to me," Aron said.

Charlie's body jostled as Noah handed her over to Aron. His warm body was pressed against hers, his heart thundered behind his ribs.

She let the sound of his heartbeat lull her into sleep.

Or maybe it was death.

Either way, she was shrouded in so much peace she never wanted to leave this place.

****

Aron sat in a chair outside of a hospital room. The hardest thing he'd done was release his hold on her so the doctors could save her life.

Hell. Releasing her long enough to get dressed before heading into civilization was fucking torture.

It had been two hours since they'd brought her here. And they hadn't heard a word from the doctors.

Hollyn, Noah, Campbell, Brax, Daxon, and Mason all sat around him, their faces full of worry. Hollyn looked downright gutted. If Charlie died, she'd lose her last remaining family.

And Aron would lose his only love. The only woman who'd claimed his heart and soul.

He would pray for death. He'd pray to follow Charlie into the afterlife if he lost her.

"She'll survive. She's a fighter," Campbell said from beside Aron.

She reached over and took his hand. He didn't have the strength to pull from her grasp. He didn't even care if it pissed Brax off. He needed the comfort. He'd even accept a hug at this point.

Charlie had done this to him. She'd made him softer. She'd made him see the world differently, had taught him love and compassion. She had shown him what true courage looked like.

Aron found out afterward what had happened. While they fought the rogues and the crows, Charlie had used her wind to create a barrier. The cowards kept dive bombing them, trying to blind them. She'd protected her mate and her friends.

And then she'd realized there was an opening to the women. She had run off on her own to rescues the prisoners. Noah, Micah, and Callie had spotted her and made sure to stick close to her side.

Good friends. Loyal friends.

Noah was right behind Charlie when she'd jerked the door open. He'd opened his mouth to warn her, but could only roar in his bear form. A loud boom echoed through the night. Then blood bloomed across the back of Charlie's shirt. The bullet had gone straight through. The doctors assured them that was a good thing. That meant they wouldn't have to dig it out.

But it also meant she bled a lot more and a lot faster.

Noah had been nicked on the shoulder by the bullet. But he'd been fine. He didn't require any medical attention.

Tears burned the back of his eyes as they waited for news. She had to make it. She had to live. He'd gladly take her place as long as she continued breathing. This world was better with her in it.

He was better with her in this fucked up world.

"Why did she run off on her own?" he muttered to himself.

No one answered. No one *had* an answer. Other than Charlie wanted to save those women from the worst kind of fate.

A doctor entered the waiting room, wiping sweat from his face with a tissue.

"Family of Charlemaine?"

"Yes," Aron said, lunging to his feet.

"I'm her cousin," Hollyn said, stepping forward.

"She's going to be fine. We stitched her up and gave her a blood transfusion. She was pretty low. Had you guys waited much longer she might not have fared so well."

The doctor's eyes scanned the room and a frown creased the skin between his brows.

"This was an accident?" he asked. He sounded skeptical.

"Yeah. We were hiking through the woods and didn't know someone was target practicing nearby," Campbell said. "Can we see her?"

The doctor looked over his shoulder then back at them. "She's being moved to a recovery room. She needs her rest. One at a time. And keep her calm. She can leave in a couple of days."

He did another look around, then lowered his voice. "And the next time you go hiking, I suggest making sure no one is aiming a gun at you." His eyes flashed amber, then faded back to their normal dark brown.

This doctor was a Shifter. How the hell had he accomplished that? How the hell had he inserted himself so far in the human world without ever being detected?

Nearly twenty minutes after the doctor left, they still hadn't heard from anyone as to where they could find Charlie and whether they could see her yet.

Aron waited impatiently, pacing from one side of the waiting room to the other, until a nurse came and told him what room to find her and reminded him to keep the visitors to one at a time.

"We'll head home. I'll check on Morse Pack and make sure everything is cool," Daxon said, clapping Aron on the shoulder.

After a brief moment, he pulled Aron into a hug, holding him tight and slapping him on the back twice before releasing him.

Aron's legs felt like they were full of lead as he took the elevator to her floor. It was like he was stuck in a dream as he made his way down the long hall to her room, but every step felt like he was still a mile away.

Finally, he made it to her door. And hesitated before walking inside.

She didn't need to see him falling apart. He needed to be strong for her. Even if he was irritated she'd taken such a risk to begin with.

Could he really fault her, though? Wouldn't he have done the same thing? Hadn't he done similar in the past in order to save someone?

Tapping lightly on the door, Aron pushed it open and peeked inside. There were no roommates. Charlie was alone. And she looked so tiny and pale in the bed.

Her eyes were closed. Tubes came from her arm and were under her nose. A steady beep came from a machine beside her bed.

Not wanting to wake her, Aron quietly lifted a chair across the room and set it beside the bed. He laid his head beside her arm and listened to her breathing, the sound reassuring.

She was alive. She'd made it. She'd been shot trying to help someone and she'd survived.

His mate was amazing.

He hadn't slept since the night before and sure as hell couldn't sleep while Charlie was fighting for her life. Now, with the beeping and the soft sound of her breaths, Aron let his eyes drift closed.

He waited for nightmares of the night before, but there was only peace. His body was exhausted.

There was no clock nearby, so Aron had no idea what time it was or how long he'd slept. But he'd woken to fingers softly threading through his hair.

Groggy brained, it took Aron a full minute to remember where he was. And then he shot straight up, his wide eyes going straight to Charlie.

She smiled at him, her eyes heavy lidded with whatever medication they'd given her for the pain.

"Hey," she said, her voice thick with sleep.

Aron leaned forward and pressed his lips to Charlie's. He didn't deepen it. Didn't touch her anywhere else. Just let his lips linger against hers as tears escaped over his lashes.

When he pulled back, Charlie had a wistful smile on her lips. "What was that for?"

"Seriously?" he said on a surprised chuckle. "I thought I was going to lose you."

Her hand raised and she pressed it against his cheek. "I'm not going anywhere."

"Charlie. You were shot." Anger rose in his chest and he fought to keep his eyes from glowing in case a nurse happened to walk in. The last thing any of them needed was for him to out the entire Shifter species. "What were you thinking? You could've been killed." He kept his voice soft. The nurse and doctor both said she had to stay calm.

"I had to get those women out. I didn't know they had a gun," she said with a shrug as if it made total sense.

Aron gaped at her. He didn't know what the hell to say to get through to her. They would've still gotten those women out if she hadn't run head first into the unknown. She had sacrificed herself for total strangers.

But that was who she was. She believed in people, saw the best in them. Even after being taken herself. She had believed James. She'd believed his story about Beth. And it had been the truth.

She had been convinced the men being forced to help the rogues in order to keep their loved ones safe wouldn't fight. And she'd been right about that, too. While they'd come barging in with the others, they had never truly fought. They'd defended themselves and each other more than anything.

And now, they were in Morse Pack territory being reunited with their wives, their sisters, and their daughters.

"Who shot me, anyway?" she asked, as she tried to sit up.

Aron held his hand out, halting her. "You're supposed to rest. Hold on." He hit the button to sit the bed up for her so she wouldn't hurt herself or rip her stitches. "It was the fourteen-year-old."

Charlie halted her movements and stared at Aron wide eyed. "Shut…up. That is *awesome*!"

"She *shot* you." Was she still loopy from the meds?

"Yeah. She was prepared to protect herself and the rest of those women. She's as bad ass as Campbell and Peyton."

"And you," he reminded her. She was, after all, sitting in a hospital bed after getting shot in the side.

"What?"

"She's as bad ass as you."

Her smile widened. "You look tired."

A grunt was all he could muster. He was bone tired. Emotionally, mentally, and physically exhausted.

But his mate was alive. She would be fine. And she would be left with a scar as a reminder of what she'd done, what she'd accomplished. She had made sure those women were out, made sure they were safe.

And once she was out of this damn hospital, he was pretty sure he'd never be more than two feet from her side for the rest of his life.

Chapter Fourteen

It had been over a month since the battle with Talonwood. Charlie had been out of the hospital and was almost completely healed.

That didn't stop Aron from doting on her and waiting on her hand and foot.

"I can do it myself," Charlie whined as she tried to put ornaments on the Christmas tree they'd brought home from the local lot.

"You need to rest," he said, batting her hands away and trying to guide her back to the couch.

Charlie firmly planted her feet in place and crossed her arms. "Okay. This has to stop. I'm fine, Aron. My stitches are out, and the doctor said I'm healing perfectly. You have to stop babying me."

He sighed heavily. Placing his hands on each of her arms, he looked down into her face. "I just don't want you to get hurt."

"I won't. I'm fine. I think it's safe to put ornaments on the tree. Not like I carried that thing in here," she teased. She would've let him carry it even if she hadn't been shot. He was far stronger than she.

His hands were warm as he rubbed them up and down her arms. "I'm trying," he confessed.

Stepping closer, Charlie wrapped her arms around Aron and tilted her head back to look into his eyes. "I know. And I appreciate it. Just…try harder," she said, shaking him as she spoke.

Aron chuckled and tightened his hold, bringing her closer so he could hug her. "I never want to lose you."

The words were so sincere and sweet. And broke her heart a bit. "You won't. I promise to never run off without back up again." She pulled back and held her fingers up like a Boy Scout.

Bending at the waist, Aron pressed his lips to hers gently. He pulled back with one of those sexy smacks and Charlie stood there with her eyes closed. She would never get tired of his lips.

"What time is everyone coming over?" she asked.

They had spent so much time in Big River territory since she'd joined the Pride, and then Morse Pack when some of the men and their family members had nowhere else to go, that she decided she wanted to host a party for once. James and Beth had spent a couple nights with Ravenwood in the beginning, but even they were now in Morse territory.

It wasn't technically a Christmas party since that was still three weeks away. It was more of a…Friendsgiving. The Pride had spent Thanksgiving together, as did the other Packs, Clans, and Prides. Now, it was time for them all to get together.

There was no way that many people would fit in her home. So, Nova had used it as an excuse to spend some money and bought a bunch of folding tables and chairs to seat everyone on Charlie's lawn. And then she had gone and bought those tall gas heaters and a bunch of tiki torches for both heat and light.

"Gray said he and the Pack would be here around four. Everyone else is coming around then, too. You sure you want to have that many people over here?"

She knew it wasn't that he thought she was still scared of Shifters. That had faded months ago. No. She knew he could feel the anxiety rolling from her of hosting her very first party ever. This was the first time since she was a child that she'd had a family or even friends to party with, after all.

"Absolutely. I can't wait."

They had bought her very first grill and set it up outside. She'd wanted to make a turkey, but with that many people, she would have had to buy at least three. So, instead, Colton and Reed offered to grill up a bunch of burgers, steaks, and hot dogs. The hot dogs were for the little girls.

"Campbell's bringing Polo, right?"

Aron shrugged. "I don't know. I can ask her. Why?"

Charlie pulled away and reached up into a cabinet in her kitchen. Pulling down a large bone, she held her hand out with a big smile. "I didn't want to leave him out of the feast."

Aron's smile grew as he shook his head. "You really do think about everyone before yourself."

"Nah. I just want Polo to like me. It's a bribe."

"He already likes you," he said, taking the bone and setting it on the table. "Everyone does."

"Good. Because I love them."

"I love you," he said, bending to press his lips to hers again. "So much."

"I love you, too."

Charlie retrieved the bone from the table and turned to put it away in the cabinet. For some reason, she wanted it to be a surprise. Not like Polo would have any idea what a surprise was, but that didn't matter.

When she turned, Aron was on one knee right there in the kitchen.

"What are you doing?" she asked, her brows pinching together.

"I know we haven't been together long. And I know our life won't be normal," he said. His Adam's apple bobbed up and down. *"We're* not normal. But I promise I'll do everything in my power to make you happy every single day for the rest of your life."

"Aron?" She was really confused now. They were already mates. He didn't have to go through all this. Her heart was already his.

He swallowed hard again and reached into his pocket. In his fingers was a simple silver band. No diamond. No intricate designs. It was perfect and so beautiful.

"I want you to be my wife. I want to marry you. I know we can't exactly go get a marriage license and all that, but I want to wake up to your beautiful face every morning. I want you to be the last thing I see before I close my eyes every night."

"You already do that." She was ruining the moment. But her thoughts were all over the place. He wanted her to marry him.

Aron could never mark her as his own the way Shifters did. So, he wanted to put a ring on her finger. He wanted the entire world to know they belonged together.

His smile was crooked and unsure as he held the ring toward her. "Will you marry me? Will you be my wife?"

Tears burned the backs of her eyes and blurred her vision. Looking down at the ring, she realized there was only one answer in the world. "Yes!" she said as she nodded over and over again. "Yes. I'll marry you. I'll be your wife."

Lowering to his level, she threw her arms around his neck and hugged him as tears spilled over her lashes.

When Aron pulled back, his own lashes were damp and his eyes were watery. He held the ring out again. Charlie offered her hand and smiled through her tears as he slipped it over her left ring finger.

"You can have any kind of wedding you want. I don't care how big or small. Anything you want, as long as I can marry you."

****

Charlie couldn't help but play with the band on her finger. Hand under the table, she kept spinning it around and around, then would smile at Aron.

It had only been a couple hours since he had dropped to one knee to ask her hand in marriage. And the excited butterflies hadn't died down since.

"You're happy today," Nova said as she balanced Rieka on her knee. The little girl kept reaching onto her momma's plate and grabbing a handful of food. Some of it went into her mouth. Some of it was dropped under the table for the big dog who sat waiting for the goodies.

Looking around the long row of tables, Charlie's heart was full.

"I am."

Everyone was there. Big River Pack. Blackwater Clan, including Colton and Shawnee. A few members of Morse Pack and the newcomers. Even some of the lionesses from Hope Pride joined them today.

A family. She had one big, strange, abnormal family and couldn't ask for more.

"How much longer?" Emory asked Shawnee as the woman rubbed her round belly.

"Days," she said as she stretched her back. "And it couldn't come soon enough. These little guys are killing my back and I don't think I've peed so much in my life."

That got a chuckle around the table.

"Have you picked out names?" Charlie asked.

Shawnee's shoulders went up in a shrug, but Colton, her mate, grinned wide. "Since we don't know whether they'll be girls or boys or both, she's got a long list of names. She said she wants to see their faces before she picks."

Colton looked down at his mate with so much love in his eyes. It was obvious he was crazy about the pregnant redhead sitting beside him.

A look around showed almost the exact same scene with every mated pair. Every male touched his female in one way or another, whether it was an arm around her shoulders, a hand on her leg, or simply sitting close enough to touch shoulder to shoulder. Or arm to shoulder as it was with some of the more petite females.

Aron was looking down at her with the same expression. Love poured from him until it took her breath away. This guy was hers. All hers. Forever and ever, until death do they part.

Well. Not quite yet. They still had to plan and go through with the ceremony.

Ducking her head, Charlie tried to get the blush she was sure painted her cheeks a bright pink to fade.

How had her life taken such a dramatic turn? How had she found these wonderful people?

How had she found such a wonderful man to be her forever love?

Once her cheeks were no longer warm, Charlie reached for the bowl of gravy to smother her mashed potatoes.

But she never made contact with the bowl.

Nova's hand shot out and grabbed hers, pulling it until Charlie was leaning over Aron as Nova examined the ring on her finger.

"Is this what I think it is?" she asked, turning wide eyes and a wider smile on Charlie.

"Depends on what you think it is," Aron answered, winking down at Charlie.

"You guys didn't get married without telling us, did you?"

"No. Nothing like that," Charlie said as her cheeks burst into flames once more.

"I asked her to marry me this morning. And she said yes."

The entire group of Shifters, Fae, and humans went silent. And then everyone erupted in cheers, whistles, and congratulations.

Females jumped from their seats and pulled Charlie up for hugs. The males nodded at Aron, gave him thumbs ups, even reached over to clap him on the shoulder.

"We've definitely got to have a bachelor party. We haven't had one for anyone yet," Reed said. Lola raised one brow at him. "No strip joints. Promise."

Aron chuckled and turned to look at Charlie. The smile on his face…all she could do was sigh as the women continued talking to her, asking to help plan the wedding, congratulating her.

All she could do was stare at the man who had embedded himself so deep in her heart she knew she would never be the same.

And she was perfectly fine with that.

This man had given her more than he could ever know. He had helped her find herself again. He had given her her cousin back.

He had given her a new family.

And someday, he'd give her a family of their very own.

Epilogue

Clint slammed his fist against the wall, his knuckles going through the drywall and making contact with a stud. Damn it. There was no chance his hand hadn't broken.

That was the least of his worries.

His entire staff had been wiped out. Maybe not all of them, but enough of them to hinder his side business.

Why the fuck did those panthers always have to get in the way? And how the fuck did they constantly find his soldiers while they were absconding with a woman? If he didn't get a few more in the books, he wouldn't get paid. And his boss would be fucking pissed.

He ought to tell the higher ups why business had been so slow lately. It wasn't his fault. He'd done everything he could to increase his numbers while making sure the crows could never be implicated.

He wasn't stupid.

The problem he had now was finding new soldiers. He had tried an old tactic and used females to blackmail assholes into working for him. There was never a shortage of fathers or brothers.

But once again, the fucking panthers ruined everything. They had gotten away with his latest cash crop and now he would have to go back to the boss empty handed.

And it hadn't been only the panthers. All their buddies had shown up. The bears. The wolves. Even the fucking lion from Tammen Pride had shown up. And he had only a handful of loyal wolf followers. The rest had surrendered the second they'd realized the massive gathering was there to help them.

Fucking useless. The whole lot of them were useless. One would think they would realize how much money was in trafficking and make a buck or two. Instead, half of them slaved away on construction sites. One of those fucking bears slopped liquor to the drunks. He didn't know what the rest of them did. And he couldn't give two shits, either.

Clint should have taken the fucking panthers out when he had the chance. They had stayed all alone in that little piece of shit trailer. He could have sent in all of Black Feather and Talonwood and annihilated them.

Now?

Now it was only the crows and a handful of Talonwood left. And the crows were no match for the panthers in human form. Their only chance would be plucking their eyeballs from their heads.

Or maybe they would make it a point to steal their women. That fucker Aron's mate was a Fairy. She hadn't done a very good job at hiding that during the battle. And the human bitch was there, too. Both of them would fetch a pretty penny.

Shit. Maybe he wouldn't stop there. Maybe he would make it his life's mission to steal every single one of the females from the Clan, the Pride, the Packs, all of them. Even those two little brats living in Big River Pack.

Oh, he was sure none of them realized he was fully aware Big River had female pups living there. He could hold onto them to make sure the Alpha and all his asshole buddies mind their business.

Okay. There was no point in dwelling on this shit. Even his hand would be healed in a day or two. He just had to rebuild. He had to find someone to do the dirty work so the crows could reap the benefits without any of the consequences.

The trouble would be finding easy targets. There was a good chance the local Shifter community would be watching the crows a lot closer. He had to find someone and make it look like their idea.

And then, he would sit back and get rich off their backs.

####

Thank you for reading ***Aron's Element***. I hope you loved Aron and Charlie as much as I do!

If you liked this book, please consider rating or reviewing it on Amazon and/or Goodreads. Your support will help other readers find the panthers, bears, and wolves of Cedar Hill!

Thank you!

To get early news, win free stuff, and enter giveaways, make sure to check out my website.

You can find it HERE!

LynnHowardBooks.com

About the Author

Lynn Howard lives in Cedar Hill, MO, where all her sexy Shifters exist. She lives and breathes hot Alpha males and sassy brassy females. She feels the most at home knee deep in mud and chicken muck and prefers to be outside under the stars, cuddled up under a blanket in front of a bonfire than in the big city.

When not typing away or feeding her chickens, you can find her fantasizing about hot country boys for her next book or wandering the woods in search of wildlife. She loves all animals and insects...except spiders. Her favorite foot accessory is barefoot and she owns at least twenty sets of salt-n-pepper shakers, yet only uses one.

Gray's Wolf is the first in the Big River Pack series. And just like in Gray's Wolf, there are more hot country boy Shifters just waiting to their turn for a little love and romance.